CINDERELLA'S BILLIONAIRE BOSS

MICHELLE DOUGLAS

Harlequin

ROMANCE

A brand-new dazzling quartet
from Harlequin Romance!

Outback Kings

Four heirs... A one-billion-dollar legacy!

In Australia's remote northwest
lies the Kimberley, home to the nation's largest
cattle station—Kings Reach. From there tycoon rancher
Fraser King runs a billion-dollar dynasty. It's his job
to protect the family legacy and he has plans
none of his four sons saw coming...

Returning home for a lavish ball honoring their late
mother, Tom, Fitz, Logan and Jack are reunited. With
them all in the same room for the first time in years,
there's no telling what drama will ensue... The only thing
for certain? Fraser's inheritance bombshell will turn the
billionaire brothers' entire lives upside down. And as for
their love lives? Well...they'll be turned inside out too!

Find out in this fabulous new miniseries:

Cinderella's Billionaire Boss by Michelle Douglas

City Girl in the Outback by Ally Blake

Stuck with Her Impossible Ex by Kandy Shepherd

The Billion-Dollar Heir Returns by Rachael Stewart

Dear Reader,

When Ally, Kandy, Rachael and I were asked to collaborate on another Australian Outback series, much happy dancing ensued (we had so much fun writing our previous one). And, voilà, the Outback Kings were born. The glorious thing about a series is it adds depth to each story—together they become more than the sum of their parts.

At the center of the Outback Kings series is a million-acre cattle station in Australia's wild and remote Kimberley, and four brothers who have forgotten how to be a family. When the future of the station is threatened, they have to decide whether to band together and fight for it *and* for each other.

Single father Tom, the second son, remembers a time when he and his brothers were close. He wants that back. Enter Charlie Ashwell, the girl next door with a heart of gold who becomes his little girl's much-needed *temporary* nanny. She's also the godsend he never knew they needed. But Charlie has secrets, and when they come to light will they destroy everything?

This story was a delight from start to finish. I hope you love our four gorgeous brothers and the fun, fierce and brave women who love them.

Hugs,

Michelle

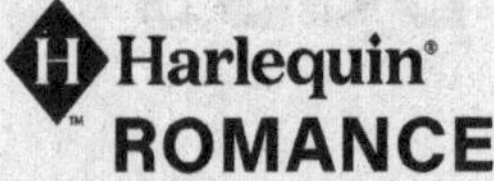

Harlequin® ROMANCE

ISBN-13: 978-1-335-47091-1

Cinderella's Billionaire Boss

Copyright © 2026 by Michelle Douglas

 Harlequin Enterprises ULC
22 Adelaide St. West, 41st Floor
Toronto, Ontario M5H 4E3, Canada
www.Harlequin.com

HarperCollins Publishers
Macken House, 39/40 Mayor Street Upper,
Dublin 1, D01 C9W8, Ireland
www.HarperCollins.com

Printed in U.S.A.

1 2 3 4 5 6 7 8 9 10 HDC 28 27 26 25

Michelle Douglas has been writing for Harlequin since 2007 and believes she has the best job in the world. She lives in a leafy suburb of Newcastle, on Australia's east coast, with her own romantic hero, a house full of dust and books, and an eclectic collection of '60s and '70s vinyl. She loves to hear from readers and can be contacted via her website, michelle-douglas.com.

Books by Michelle Douglas

Harlequin Romance

One Summer in Italy

Unbuttoning the Tuscan Tycoon
Cinderella's Secret Fling

One Year to Wed

Claiming His Billion-Dollar Bride

Summer Escapes

The Venice Reunion Arrangement

Wedding Date in Malaysia
Reclusive Millionaire's Mistletoe Miracle
Waking Up Married to the Billionaire
Tempted by Her Greek Island Bodyguard
Secret Fling with the Billionaire
Tempted by Her Best Friend Billionaire
Forbidden Cinderella in His Castello

Visit the Author Profile page
at Harlequin.com for more titles.

To the irrepressible forces of nature that are
Ally Blake, Kandy Shepherd and Rachael Stewart. Your
humor, your cool competence and "can do" attitudes
have made writing this series an absolute joy.

PROLOGUE

Thomas Benedick King's forebears wouldn't recognise the barn. Hung with glittering chandeliers, the rafters and support beams draped in ivy and fairy lights, and every table boasting a tasteful candle, it languidly proclaimed itself the epitome of rustic sophistication. A far cry from the barn he and his brothers used play basketball in during the wet season.

Tom—who only felt like he lived up to his full name when he was home on the station, dressed in a penguin suit with a glass of champagne in hand, which admittedly wasn't all that often—moved towards the shadows at the side of the room. Not that all of this gleaming, sparkling light left room for shadows. At least not the kind you could see.

Not true. He could see them flit across his brothers' faces when they didn't know he was watching. They could probably see them in his. If he looked he might even see them in his father's. *If* he looked.

While there might not be actual shadows to

darken the room, palms in enormous planters had been placed at strategic intervals and he made for one of those now, breathed in the green to clear his lungs. The multitude of diamonds and gems that glittered at elegant throats and wrists, the designer dresses, designer watches, designer scents, all competing with each other, made his temples throb.

The official part of the evening was over— the speeches honouring the Eliza King Foundation had been made. His mother's tireless support had helped fund the Flying Doctor service, the School of the Air, annual school camps for children of the Kimberley, and had assisted vulnerable women and children in the region. *Everyone* wanted to pay homage to her.

An invisible fist closed about Tom's chest and squeezed. *Ten years.* His mother had been gone for a decade. It still felt wrong.

Surreptitiously emptying his glass of fizz into the planter, he folded his arms and leaned back. Eliza would've loved all of this—the flamboyant sophistication, the chance to play society hostess and showcase her beautiful home, the ten-piece band playing big-band numbers.

Everywhere he looked he saw Australia's high fliers—politicians, business people, celebrities— interspersed here and there with the odd international guest of note. The King name carried kudos and everyone wanted to be seen at the event of the season.

The station's airfield currently boasted a veritable fleet of private planes and helicopters while every bedroom in the Federation homestead—a two-storey monstrosity—was occupied. Fitz's eco-accommodation was bursting at the seams and glamping tents had been set up on the lush south lawn.

Bespoke. Extravagant. Over-the-top. And Eliza would've loved it. But what she'd have loved most was having all four of her boys under the same roof again.

With a speed born of practice, he zeroed in on each of his brothers. Two Federal politicians had waylaid Jack, the eldest, who took tall, dark and brooding to an entirely new level. They were probably attempting to canvas his support. *Yeah, good luck with that.*

Fitz, now the youngest, radiating outdoorsy energy with his tan, his sun-kissed hair and lean-muscled fitness, stood with a group of station managers. They were probably grilling him on the success of his ecotourism business, hungering to emulate it.

Logan, son number three, who stood head and shoulders above ninety-nine per cent of people in the room, gestured animatedly. A group of women gazed at him adoringly, and Tom huffed out a laugh. Knowing Logan, he probably hadn't noticed. He was probably too busy outlining ways to save the world.

And here *he* was—the second son—hiding behind a potted palm.

Not hiding. Taking a breather. His daughter, Bea, had hauled him out of bed at five am, her five-year-old body squirming with excitement at being on the station. 'Daddy, wake up! I want to see the horses and the cows and the dogs and the unicorns.'

He smothered a yawn, noted that Jack had edged closer to one of the exits, and kicked his exhaustion to the kerb. He'd sleep later.

A drinks tray passed across his line of vision. Perched on it was a single glass of beer, moisture condensing on its sides. His eyes followed it. His mouth watered. He could murder one of those.

As if by magic, the glass came to a halt in front of him. 'I noticed you'd finished your champagne.' The flute was plucked from his fingers and a glance directed at the planter. Blue eyes danced when they lifted again and a mobile mouth stretched in a wide grin. 'Never fear, your secret is safe with me.'

He grinned back, couldn't seem to help it. She wore the uniform of the catering detail, black trousers and crisp white shirt, which was a shame. A bit of light banter and harmless flirtation was exactly what he needed. Emphasis on the light and harmless though. It wouldn't be fair to distract her while she was working.

She presented the beer to him like a prize. 'I thought you might like one of these.'

'That obvious?' He seized the beer and took a long swig. 'Why aren't you circulating trays of these around the room?'

She leaned in closer as if confiding a secret. 'Apparently it's not the right *tone*.'

She smelled of vanilla and eucalyptus drops. Innocent. Wholesome. His body shifted, tightened. Nothing innocent and wholesome about that.

She nodded to the beer, and everything about her briefly *twinkled*. As if she were Tinkerbell! 'Enjoy!'

She turned, probably to go to load up her tray with discarded glasses, and he couldn't help noticing the sweet curve of her backside. 'Why'd I get the special treatment?'

She glanced back, brows lifting. 'Nothing's too good for the princes of the realm.'

She knew who he was, then.

She winked. 'And I thought it might give you a second wind.'

'Ah, an angel of mercy—'

From the corner of his eye he caught Jack slipping out of the side door. If his brother left without saying a word ag*ain*… Catching Logan's eye, he hitched his head at the door. Logan immediately excused himself from his group and set off in Jack's wake.

'Tom?'

He glanced down to find his angel of mercy

frowning at him. He set his beer back on her tray. 'Sorry. Something I need to take care of.'

Moving outside, he seized his phone and texted Fitz.

Fitz appeared a moment later. 'What's up?'

'Jack's on the move.'

As soon as they left the light of the barn behind, the tightness in Tom's chest eased and he filled his lungs with the scent of the Kimberley. Ahead of them Logan moved without hesitation, and beyond him Tom could just make out the dark shape of Jack. All four of them were moving towards their old haunt—the waterhole. For the first time in over twenty years.

Glancing at a dark sky liberally sprinkled with stars, he nodded once. Hard. *This*. They'd been close once. Brothers. He wanted that back.

And tonight that felt possible.

Huffing out a laugh, he grabbed Fitz in a playful headlock to knuckle his skull the way he had when they were boys. Except his knuckles barely made it anywhere near Fitz's skull before he found himself in an armlock that threatened to have him face first in the dirt.

'Mum will be pissed if you mess up the tux!' he shouted, choking back a laugh.

It had been the refrain his brothers had flung at Tom—ever the joker—as kids, and it had Fitz hooting out a laugh now as he released him. Holy cow! His little brother had been eye-wateringly fast. And strong.

'Stop messing about, you two,' Logan growled from up ahead.

Tom and Fitz shared a look. Tom raised an eyebrow. Fitz nodded. With whoops, they raced forward to jostle and shoulder him, threatening to tackle him to the ground until he too was laughing and crying, 'Uncle!'

Fitz chuckled. 'You two are getting soft.'

'Soft?' He feigned affront. 'I'll have you know I go star wrangling and unicorn hunting on a regular basis.'

'Man, that kid is the best.' Fitz's grin became a little goofy.

Bea and Fitz had taken one look at each other and—*bam!*—utterly besotted. Logan would walk over hot coals for his niece. And now so would Fitz. *Mission accomplished.*

With arms casually slung over one another's shoulders and still jostling each other, they arrived at the waterhole. To find Jack standing motionless, staring at the water.

Tom's hands clenched and unclenched. He wanted Bea to have uncles she could rely on. He wanted Jack among their number. His daughter *deserved* family.

Except Jack had halted beneath *Will's* tree. When he reached up to curl a hand around the branch above, the air in Tom's lungs jammed. Jack had built Will a treehouse in those branches— a place for their youngest brother to avoid their father's constant haranguing. Acid burned his stomach. After Will's death, their father had torn it down.

Fitz broke away to veer in the opposite direction, the way he swiped at the heads of Mitchell grass betraying his inner turmoil. Even after all this time, the loss of his twin bit deep. Logan followed after him, halting a good twelve feet to Jack's right.

Tom shoved his hands in his pockets and forced his feet in Jack's direction. He'd been fourteen when Jack had left, but Fitz had only been nine, and Logan eleven. 'You lot remember the hours we spent down here—the swimming, the water fights…all of us ganging up on Jack to dunk him.' Jack had always been the biggest and strongest. 'Together we could manage it now too if we took him off guard.'

Nobody laughed. The air was heavy enough to sink all of them.

'The hours we spent plotting in Will's tree-house… The strategy meetings—how to smuggle fireworks in without Dad finding out; how to build the biggest water bomb; how to be included on an overnight muster.'

It was as if his was the only voice on the air. It wasn't. The night was alive with the sound of frogs, insects and night birds. It was a sound that soothed his soul when he hadn't realised it needed soothing. It was good to be back.

He hitched his chin at the scene in front of

them. 'That was twenty years ago, but this place is still magic.'

He moved to the high edge of the waterhole—their favourite launchpad when practising dive-bombs—all of them trying to outdo one another. He half-hoped Jack would lean forward and push him in—an all-in water fight would break the tension that bound them tight. He could work with a prank, with playfulness, with laughter. He might then have a chance of turning the four of them into a family again.

God forbid, but if something should ever happen to him...

It was pointless pretending it couldn't. It had happened to Will. And it had happened to Madeline, his late wife. He needed to surround his daughter with love and provide her with people she could turn to if the worst ever did happen. He *needed* his brothers to be those people.

'I should've snagged a bottle of champagne and some glasses. But... Let's have a toast anyway.' He lifted his hand in the air as if raising a glass.

'What are we toasting?' Logan lifted his hand too.

'To Mum. Miss you to bits. And to Will. Wish you were here, bud.' If he'd had a glass of bubbles, he'd have downed it in one.

Stars reflected in the still water in front of them and a tawny frogmouth swooped through the air with barely a rustle. 'I've had a few people say tonight that they wonder what kind of man Will would've become.' Three sets of eyes turned to him. 'We all know what kind of man he'd have been. A good man.' He paused. 'What I wonder, though, is what he'd have made of all of us now?'

'Are you interested in knowing what I make of all of you now?'

A voice of gravel broke across the night air, shattering the delicate circle of brotherhood that had started to form. Tom was the last to turn.

Their father assessed each of them in turn—Fitz, Logan, Tom… Jack—and shook his head. 'Why am I not surprised to find you *all* down here?'

The way Fraser emphasised *all* had Tom glancing across at Jack. Had he arranged to meet their father? Were bridges being mended? His lips twisted. Were the rest of them in the way?

'Were you hoping to find someone in particular?' Tom drawled.

'It's fortuitous to have found you *all*.'

Which wasn't an answer to the question.

'I've something to tell you, and now is as good a time as any.' Fraser planted his hands on his hips. 'I've thought about this long and hard, but I've come to a decision and have hired lawyers.'

Logan stiffened. '*I'm* the station's lawyer.'

'In this instance you've a vested interest.'

What the hell…?

'I'm starting proceedings to break the irrevocable trust.'

Tom's head rocked back. The trust had been

put into place after their mother's death—she'd made Fraser promise it on her deathbed. It left Kings Reach and its associated holdings equally to all four surviving sons. And Fraser wanted to *break* it?

Logan jabbed a finger skywards. 'You *can't* break an irrevocable trust. *That's* the point. I know. I'm the one who drafted it.'

Fraser widened his stance. 'We'll see.'

Logan shook himself. 'What do you want to replace it with?'

'I plan to leave the entire management of Kings Reach to Jack.'

To Jack. Every feeling of inadequacy from Tom's childhood came roaring to the fore now. He'd never been good enough for his father. *Never.*

Fraser thrust out his chin. 'This is what your mother would've wanted.'

That was a lie.

Jack gave a harsh laugh. 'Do you care about your legacy so little you'd leave it to the one man who'd see it divided up and sold off to the highest bidder?'

The words chilled Tom to his marrow.

Fraser's nostrils flared. 'When you get down to it, it's just real estate. And real estate is your superpower, Jack.'

Nobody spoke. Nothing moved.

'None of you will now be surprised when you receive the paperwork from my lawyers.'

Turning back in the direction of the party, Fraser walked away. Without halting, without looking back, without explaining.

CHAPTER ONE

CHARLIE STARED AT the glass of beer on her tray with the single mouthful taken from it, and then after the man who'd placed it there. A sigh of appreciation rose through her. Hot damn, but Tom King had the lean-hipped, broad-shouldered swagger of an outback cowboy.

He's not a cowboy, though. He's not a country boy.

Exactly. And she had no intention of forgetting it. The fact he retained the aura meant nothing. It had been bred into him by the previous five generations of outback Kings, that was all. Though she defied any woman not to find it attractive. Tom King was six feet four of lean, muscular power and it left her breasts tingling and a strange restlessness fidgeting through her blood.

'He could be a girl's best worst mistake,' Grace murmured in her ear, her tray of empty glasses balanced perfectly.

She and Grace watched Tom disappear through the French doors. 'Ain't that the truth?' Except

Charlie wasn't interested in making any kind of mistakes—fun or otherwise—with a city boy.

'Interested?'

She sent Grace a mock glare. 'Absolutely not.'

Grace grinned. They'd been besties since their School of the Air days. 'Liar, liar, pants on fire.'

Laughter bubbled from her throat. 'He's just pretty to look at. And...'

'And?'

'It's funny but I don't remember him.'

Obviously she *knew* of the four brothers—the King family were Kimberley royalty. She didn't remember Jack—she'd have only been eight or nine when he'd left Kings Reach—but she and Fitz had been in the same year when they were doing School of the Air, which meant they'd chatted on the radio, had met up at the arranged socials—on show days and race days and whatnot. And Logan too. She remembered him. He'd danced with her at a ball once. But she didn't recall Tom. She had a feeling that if she'd ever met him she'd have never forgotten him.

Grace shrugged. 'He's six or seven years older than us and ran with a different crowd. By the time the rest of us girls were mooning over the King boys, you'd met Connor and had eyes for no one else.'

Connor's name traced a path of ice down her spine. Charlie straightened. 'We're next-door neighbours. It seems wrong not to have met one another.'

'He hasn't been your neighbour for fifteen years.'

'Good point.' Tom had moved to Sydney. And he rarely visited.

'And, while you might be neighbours, it *is* five hours' drive from door-to-door.'

'Another excellent point. It's a bit far for popping across for a cup of sugar.'

'You'd need to be making a seriously important cake if you were.'

Both women laughed and Charlie got back to work. Noticing as she did that Fraser also exited through a side-door—the same one Tom had.

A hot fist of rage squeezed her heart. Fraser King held himself up as a figure of unimpeachable respectability, but he had all the integrity of cheap shoe leather. He was a liar and a cheat and she'd get the proof of it if it was the last thing she did. And once she had it, she'd confront him and force him to do the right thing. Or expose him for the snake he was.

Breathe, Charlie, breathe.

Loosening her grip on her tray, she continued her rounds, keeping the smile firmly pasted on her face. Taking the empty glasses back to the kitchen—the homestead shared a covered walkway with the barn—she seized a fresh tray of sparkling, fizzing flutes. There were faces here tonight she'd only seen on TV. If her mind wasn't so focused on what she was about to do, she might've enjoyed this glimpse into how the other half lived.

'Time to take your break, Charlie,' the catering manager called out.

Her heart gave a giant kick. It took all of her concentration to lower the tray back to the bench without dropping it. *This* was the moment she'd been waiting for.

Moving out through the opposite door, instead of turning left to the staff's allocated break-room she cast a quick glance around—not a soul in sight—and turned right to make her way further inside the Kings Reach homestead. She tried to look unhurried, tried to look innocent. If someone called out to her, she wanted it to look like an accident.

The moment she rounded the corner, she flattened herself against the wall and pressed a hand to her racing heart. *Breathe, Charlie, breathe.*

On the wall opposite was an Albert Namatjira painting. Good lord, was that an original? She leaned forward. It was exquisite and—

Focus!

She shook herself.

And don't bump into anything.

The house was a veritable Aladdin's cave of beautiful things. That little vase on the side-table was probably worth her annual salary. She patted her chest, ordered her heart to stop pounding.

Right, if her intel was correct, she needed to take the dog-leg at the end of this corridor—left and then a quick right. That corridor would then lead her to the front of the house with its grand foyer. Fraser's office was the second door on the right.

She didn't stop to admire the elegant Federation lines of the grand homestead with its rich wooden panelling and pressed-tin ceilings, or the tessellated tiles in rich hues of terracotta, cream and green that made a fancy pattern beneath her feet. She kept her gaze carefully averted from the picture rail hung with paintings from world-renowned artists, and the antique pendant lights that bathed it all in a warm glow. She did her best to ignore the beautiful antique furniture, because if she let herself pause for just a moment she feared she'd lose herself in the wonder of it all.

She had to focus on what was important—finding the contract Fraser had reneged on, and then forcing him to honour it. A lump lodged in her throat. She *had* to make him do the right thing. Her grandfather had brought in the new stock in good faith—it'd taken most of Melaleuca Downs's available funds, but as a family they'd agreed it was worth the risk. Increasing the size of the herd would keep them afloat. But for Fraser to renege on the deal at the last minute and refuse to lease them the promised parcel of land…

She clenched her hands so hard they hurt. Pop had turned grey when he'd received the news. She blinked back hot tears. If one more thing went wrong—a single contract lost, an outbreak of pests or disease, the wet season arriving too late or staying too long—Melaleuca would slide into a spiral of debt and bankruptcy and they'd lose everything.

She'd seen it happen to Grace's family four years ago. The McKinleys had lost their station two years ago, and rumour had it that the Buchanans were going to be next. She couldn't let Melaleuca Downs join their ranks. Her grandfather deserved an easy retirement, deserved to see out his days on the land he loved. If they lost everything—

A wave of dizziness gripped her, and she had to brace her hands on her knees. *Breathe, Charlie, Breathe.* Losing Melaleuca would tear the heart from her chest, but she was young enough to start again. So was her mother. But Nan and Pop?

Gritting her teeth, she straightened. She couldn't let that happen. Not when there was something she could do about it. Pop had taught her everything there was to know about station management and how to survive on the land if she was ever lost. More importantly, he'd taught her the value of honesty, integrity and fighting for what was right.

And Fraser reneging on the contract *wasn't* right.

Stepping into the grand foyer, she counted doors. That one was Fraser's office door. Not a speck of light showed from beneath and not a sound whispered from behind it. Holding her breath, she reached for the door handle—

'What are you doing?'

She should've jumped ten feet, except…that was a child's voice.

Abort mission.

Glancing up, she spotted a little head peeking over the balustrade and found herself smiling. Horses, dogs, kids—she was a sucker for the lot of them. 'Hello, there. I think I know who you are.'

'You do?'

She ambled around to the base of the stairs. 'You're Bea,' everyone knew Tom had a daughter, 'and I bet you're a secret fairy-tale princess. I've always wanted to meet one of those.'

Bea giggled. 'I'm not a princess.'

'I bet your daddy thinks you are.' She sat on the third stair from the bottom. She didn't want to scare Bea—stranger danger and all that—but what was this poppet doing up at this hour of the night?

'Do you know my daddy?'

'Well, I know who he is, but I don't actually *know* him. I know your Uncle Fitz, though.'

The child scampered down the stairs and planted herself on the stair beside Charlie. 'Isn't Uncle Fitz the best!'

Ooh, there was some major hero worship happening here. 'He is one cool dude.'

'One cool dude,' Bea repeated as if memorising it.

Charlie seriously hoped she was present when Bea used it on her uncle the first time. 'And I'm Charlie.'

'Why aren't you in a party dress?'

'Because I'm a waitress not a partygoer. This is my waitressing uniform.'

Bea plunked a glum chin in her hands. 'A waitress?'

She bit back a laugh. Bea made it sound like a fate worse than death. 'I'll have you know I'm not just *any* waitress. I'm a waitress *extraordinaire*. I can balance twelve full glasses of champagne on my tray in one hand like this—' she demonstrated '—and walk from one end of the ballroom to the other without spilling a single drop.'

Bea straightened. 'I want to do that.'

'It's fun. But you need to start small, use plastic glasses to begin with, until you get the hang of it.'

Bea practised holding her hand the same way Charlie had.

'I'm supposed to be on my break.' Charlie scratched her head. 'I'm supposed to be making a cup of tea and having a toilet break—that was the plan—but I took a wrong turn.'

'It's a really big house.'

'It is. It's a funny thing though, Bea. When I'm outside where it's even bigger than this house, I can navigate by the stars.'

'What does that mean?'

'It means I can look at the sky and the stars tell me where I need to go. I could get from here to my house, which is five hours away by car, just by following the stars. But when I'm inside, I lose all sense of direction.'

'Because you can't see the stars?' Bea stared at her with enormous eyes. 'Can you teach me how to do that too?'

'I bet your dad could teach you. Your Uncle Fitz certainly could. And don't forget, he's…'

'A cool dude!' Bea succumbed to a fit of the giggles, and at that very moment the front door flew open and both Bea and Charlie swung to stare as Tom stormed in with a face like a storm cloud.

'Daddy!'

A storm cloud that immediately evaporated when he spotted his daughter. It turned Charlie's insides into a huge great mushy mess. Tom looked at Bea as if she was every fairy-tale princess, unicorn and rainbow he'd ever seen all rolled into one—and her heart thump-thumped and her pulse clap-clapped, and her skin drew tight. He caught Bea easily as she flung herself at him. Nice arms. Nice throat too now that the tie and top button were undone.

'This is Charlie and she can read the stars and balance twelve glasses on a tray and I want to do that too.'

Tom raised an eyebrow in Charlie's direction. She stood, her belly fluttering in some silly schoolgirl fashion she was determined to ignore. 'I took a wrong turn…'

'Because she can't see the stars inside,' Bea added in case he hadn't been able to work that out for himself.

'And when I spotted Bea—'

'I saw you first.'

'Very true! Well, anyway, we decided to make each other's acquaintance.' She glanced at her watch. 'But my break is up. Time for me to get back to work.'

He stared at her for a moment and then to the spot on the stairs where they'd been sitting. 'Thank you, for…'

'No probs.' She edged away. With his little girl tucked up safe in his arms, Tom King looked super-deliciously and dangerously attractive. And she had to stop looking because she and Tom were chalk and cheese. Guys like him didn't have room in their lives for girls like her. And she'd do well to remember it.

'Wait, Charlie,' Bea called after her. 'You didn't tell me how to know if I'm a secret fairy princess.'

'That's because it's a tricky business working something like that out and I have to get back to work now, but I bet your daddy knows.'

He'd started up the stairs, but halted to shoot her a 'thank you very much' glare. One corner of his mouth hooked up, though, and she swore his eyes danced.

'You didn't get your cup of tea,' Bea stage-whispered.

Charlie bit back a grin at Bea's classic delaying tactics. 'I'll sneak one in, never fear. Night-night, Bea.'

'Night-night, Charlie.'

The next morning—early—Tom met Logan in the breakfast room.

'Jack's gone,' Logan said without preamble.

His lips twisted. Of course he had. 'You get a chance to talk to him?'

'Nope. Haven't spoken to Fitz either. He's already out—' he gestured outside '—God only knows where.'

Tom swore. In an ideal world all four of them would be sitting down and having a free and frank discussion. But even if all four of them were here, he wasn't sure that was possible. He stared out of the window at the sky that had only just started to lighten. Unbidden, an image of Charlie waking rose through his mind—those blue eyes of hers heavy with sleep and those blonde curls tousled—

He shook himself, banished the images. Right. Jack was currently out of their reach, but Fitz...

He understood his younger brother's need to mull things over under a wide-open sky, but of the four of them Fitz had the most to lose, and there was strength in numbers. 'Give him some time to get his head around it. Fraser's bombshell was a jaw-dropper.'

Logan's eyes blazed. 'This whole situation sucks! It's unfair and unjust. And it's *not* going to happen.'

'But—'

'It's an irrevocable trust, Tom. *Irrevocable.* That's the point of it—it *can't* be changed.'

Tom poured them coffees, handed one to Logan. 'You have the legal knowledge and I believe you. But Fraser always liked to set a precedent, and there's no denying he's got a bee in his bonnet about this, which means he's going to be stubborn. *That* means he'll throw a lot of resources at it.'

Logan's mouth firmed. 'We have a lot of resources ourselves. We fight back.'

'You bet. In the meantime we work on ensuring the press don't get hold of the story.'

'God, yes.' Logan swallowed. 'Do you trust me to—?'

'I trust you with my life, mate.' He clapped his brother on the shoulder. 'I trust you with Bea's.' And as far as he was concerned there was no greater tribute. 'And I trust you to take the lead on the legal side of things.' He sipped his coffee. 'I have a lot of resources—money. All of it is at your disposal.'

A look passed between them, loaded with history and memory and meaning. All Logan said, though, was, 'Thanks, Tom.'

They finished their coffees in silence and Logan immediately topped them up. If Tom kept drinking coffee at this rate he'd be as buzzy and fizzy as Bea. That didn't stop him from taking another sip.

'Do you trust Jack? What side of the fight is he going to fall on?'

Tom wanted to say yes, but…

Logan's lips thinned at whatever he saw in Tom's face.

'I don't know.' He had to force the words out. Once upon a time… But once upon a time was a long time ago. 'Maybe neither.' A chasm opened in his chest. Jack had walked away from all of them twenty years ago. He might not want to come back.

If I had the chance, I'd burn Kings Reach to the ground. Jack had been reported as saying that in the papers. If control of the station passed to him, what was to stop him from making good on his threat? He could decide to build a whopping great luxury hotel out here. It was what he did— build extraordinary hotels. He could do away with Fitz's ecotourism business.

'What about Fitz?' Logan persisted.

'I'd trust Fitz with my life.' He said it without hesitation.

'Not what I meant. Fraser has let him down too many times. This could be the proverbial straw.'

His heart gave a painful kick. 'You're worried he'll walk away?' A moment later he shook his head. 'Remember what a bolshie brat he was? Justice and fairness were always big things for him. If he thought he was being left out of something, he'd march right up to us—and anyone else for that matter—and let us know it wasn't fair.'

Logan gave a hollow laugh. 'Yeah, to everyone except Dad.'

Tom swore. 'Look, I'll do what I can to sort things out here. You go and tackle the legal stuff. I'll talk to Fitz—' He'd pin his brother down somehow '—and I'll try to talk sense into Fraser.'

'What about work? You're flat out.'

'I'll offload what I can.' He had a good team. 'The rest I'll juggle remotely.'

'And Bea?'

'School of the Air. I'll oversee her lessons.'

'That's a lot, Tom. Especially when you factor in trying to talk to Fraser and pinning Fitz down.' Humour momentarily lit Logan's eyes. 'I think I'm getting the better end of the deal.'

Tom laughed. 'We need you focused on the legal stuff. Don't worry about me. This is one battle Fraser *isn't* going to win.'

Logan left. Tom pulled out his phone and accessed the group chat the four brothers used— *rarely* used.

Fitz and Jack, check in ASAP. Logan and I have a game plan.

And then because he wanted to lighten the moment and ached for the sense of solidarity they'd once shared, he attached a meme of four young boys hanging intently over a game board, and hit send.

He wondered how many other messages he'd have to send before Fitz and Jack responded. He squared his jaw. He'd send as many as he had to.

By the time Monday evening rolled around, Tom couldn't believe he had any hair left. Bea had woken him at the crack of dawn, jumping on him as if he were a trampoline, demanding to see the horses, the dogs, the cows—*again*. When she'd learned she'd be spending the morning at 'school', she'd thrown a hissy fit of monumental proportions.

He knew it was a combination of things—excitement, overtiredness, disappointment at not seeing as much of her Uncle Fitz these past couple of days as she'd hoped…and puzzlement with her grandfather and the fact he barely spoke to her. She had his full sympathy on those last two.

He'd reconciled her to the idea of school, though it had taken longer than it normally would, and he'd promised to take her down to the waterhole afterwards and regale her with stories from when he was a boy, but his meeting had run over time. The housekeeper, Mrs McRae, had stepped into the breach. She'd been the housekeeper back when Tom was a boy and her no-nonsense common sense was exactly what both he and Bea needed. Bea, though, had wanted to run and jump and whoop—not help make lunch.

After they'd eaten he'd taken her down to the waterhole—had let her run and jump and whoop to her heart's content. He'd taken her to see the horses, the dogs, the cows. They'd had mock races, played tag and I Spy. He'd hoped to run her so ragged she'd collapse in a heap. Instead he was the one ready to collapse. Setting Bea up with colouring books and crayons at the kitchen table, he asked Mrs McRae to keep an eye on her while he made a quick phone call.

Damn it. Things weren't going to plan. Fitz had been elusive, while Fraser had greeted Tom's announcement that he was staying with a brooding silence. He hadn't found a way to get the older man alone either. Several guests had stayed on over the weekend and Fraser had busied himself with them.

Fraser said good morning to Bea at breakfast, he asked her how her day was going in the afternoon, and he said goodnight to her when she went upstairs in the evening. That was the extent of his engagement with his granddaughter. It was more than he gave to Tom. Not that Tom cared—he was a grown-up. 'He makes no effort with her,' he grumbled to Logan on the phone now. 'Yesterday she asked me why he didn't like her.' He'd smoothed that over, but still…

'I asked you the same question once.'

He had?

'Fact is, he is clueless without Mum.'

Tom rubbed a hand over his face. 'I'll do what I can to pin him and Fitz down in the next couple of days.'

When Tom walked into the kitchen, Mrs McRae sent him a *look* that left him in no doubt that her babysitting duties were at an end—period. She pointed. Bea had scribbled all over the benchtop in blue and red crayon.

Smothering something impatient, he grabbed the kitchen cleanser, sprayed the area liberally, and handed Bea a cloth and pointed. Her bottom lip jutted out and she kicked her stool, but she obeyed his silent instruction. 'You know better than that, Beatrice.'

He only called her Beatrice when he was seriously miffed. Her bottom lip wobbled. He wanted to swear. He wanted to roar. He wanted to *sleep*.

'As the tension in this place is stretching my nerves thin,' Mrs McRae said as he put the cleanser away, 'can't say I blame the littlie.'

He briefly closed his eyes. He wasn't winning any father-of-the-year awards today, that was for sure. Bea thrived on routine—a routine that had been completely upended these last few days. No doubt she'd also picked up on his tension—the anger and frustration he'd done his best to hide. She was only five years old. He needed to do better.

Blowing out a breath, he straightened. He *would* do better. Starting with a change of scenery. 'What if Bea and I eat down at the rec club tonight?'

The older woman dusted off her hands. 'Excellent idea.'

'You've been a saint today, Mrs Mac.'

'Don't expect this to be repeated tomorrow, Tom. I've enough work to do, and I'm too old for youngsters these days.'

'I'll sort something out,' he promised.

But what? He couldn't pass off any more of his clients. He couldn't *not* spend time with Bea. And he still needed to find out where Fitz's head was at—he needed his brother to know that he and Logan stood beside him. *And* he needed to work on their father.

Yeah, fat chance. The only one of them that had ever had any influence on Fraser was Jack. And who the hell knew what Jack's reaction—or role—in any of this was? But he had to at least try and make Fraser see sense.

'What's a rec club?' Bea asked, as they strolled down the road that continued past the homestead to where the rec club was located. A little further along, hidden behind a screen of emu apple trees and weeping bottlebrush, were the staff quarters and dining hall.

'It's a place where all the people who work on the station can go to relax. It has an inside bit and an outside bit. There's a pool table and a dartboard and you can buy drinks and food. It's nice.'

He opened the door and ushered her through and Bea's face immediately lit up. 'Charlie!'

She raced over to the bar and clambered up onto a tall stool. 'Are you being a waitress again?'

'Hiya, Bea. Nope, today I'm a *barmaid*.'

'What do you have to do?'

Charlie flashed Tom a grin as he took the stool beside Bea's. 'I make the drinks, serve the food and take the money.' She leaned across the bar and winked. 'In here, I'm the boss. At least for tonight. We take it in turns.'

Bea slumped on the bar. 'I want to be boss.' She straightened again. 'Is it more fun than being a waitress?'

'Different fun.'

Charlie set a beer in front of Tom and he blinked, his lips twisting into a wry grin at the sympathetic humour in her eyes. 'Is it that obvious ag*ain*?'

'Only because I'm a barmaid extraordinaire.' She placed a bright red drink in front of Bea. 'And a special drink for Princess Bea—a fire engine.'

Tom sipped his beer and tried not to groan. He was dog tired, which meant he should probably avoid alcohol, but it was one drink and he felt as if he'd earned it.

As Bea and Charlie chattered away like a pair of rainbow lorikeets, he found himself slowly relaxing. Bea's giggles and Charlie's easy manner wrapped him in an oasis of calm he hadn't realised he'd been craving. A sense of calm he hadn't even thought possible here at Kings Reach.

He came to when a shapely hand tapped the bar in front of him, the fingers and thumb brushing together in a silent demand that he pay up. He fought back a laugh. This wasn't a woman who'd let a person's status intimidate her into giving them a free ride. He paid up.

'Keep the change. We'll want dinner too.' The rec club was a cooperative formed and managed by the station workers. Any profits made went back into the club for improvements and to subsidise the food and drinks. There wasn't a lot of social life out here in the Kimberley, but he was happy to support what little there was. A place like this where people could come for some R&R, to let off some steam…to not be alone or feel isolated, was a godsend.

He eased back when he realised Charlie had set Bea up with a stack of napkins that his daughter was very carefully folding. He stared at Bea and then at Charlie and raised both hands in silent question. How had she taken his grumpy, out-of-sorts five-year-old and turned her into this vision of contented industry?

Charlie winked. 'I hope you don't mind, but I've co-opted Bea into helping me out.'

Mind? He could kiss her!

Things inside him shifted at the thought. *Settle.*

He reached for a napkin but Bea took it from

him. 'This is *my* job. Charlie said *I'm* second boss. You can be third boss if you want.'

He bit back the laugh that would've offended his daughter deeply. 'Why don't I settle for just being a happy customer?'

Bea nodded, satisfied that the current status quo wouldn't be upset, and set to folding more napkins.

Charlie wiped down the bar. 'Bit of a day, huh?'

'You could say that.' And then he found himself telling her in half-sentences and eye-rolls all about it. And she kept up with it effortlessly. As if she was used to inarticulate males. It felt nice to share it with someone. It felt good—

He froze with his glass halfway to his mouth. He glanced at Bea. He glanced at Charlie. He needed help with Bea. Bea had bonded with Charlie. And Charlie was great with her.

Could *Charlie* be the solution he was looking for?

CHAPTER TWO

Everything about Tom sharpened and Charlie watched in fascination. She fancied she could see the cogs in his brain turning. He might look laconic and easy-going with his loose-hipped, long-legged stride and his not-so-slow lopsided grin—a grin wide and full of humour—but behind all of that she sensed a fierce intelligence.

Duh. He had to be intelligent. He'd established a mega-successful financial consulting firm. Apparently the crème de la crème of Australian movers and shakers were among his clients. From all accounts, though, he couldn't be drawn into namedropping. But after meeting him, Tom didn't strike her as the kind of guy who needed to brag. He was a man utterly comfortable in his own skin and his place in the world.

Double duh. He was a King of Kings Reach. Confident was how they bred them. And when that skin was as smokin' hot as…

She dragged her gaze away. Not looking. She wasn't going to weave fantasies about any of the King boys.

Not even short-term ones?

Oh, stop it. What was she—sixteen?

You're not as old as you make yourself out to be.

Filling a glass with water, she set it in front of Tom. From what he'd just told her, he hadn't stopped all day. He needed to keep hydrated. Things inside her jumped when she found him watching her so closely, though.

He leant an elbow on the bar. 'What job do you normally do?'

Those grey eyes could focus on a person with the same concentration that her pack of muster dogs did when waiting for her to give them a command. Shivers rippled through her. Reaching for the water, she poured a glass for herself too. 'I'm a woman of action, Tom, not a cowpat.'

It was something Pop always said and it had Tom choking out a laugh. She shrugged. 'I'm a Jill of all trades.' She said it as if being a Jill of all trades was the best thing in the world, which it kind of was.

He stared at her mouth as if it fascinated him. She seized her water and gulped down a huge mouthful, praying it'd help her cool off. 'But mostly I'm a stockwoman extraordinaire and the best weaner educator this side of Halls Creek.'

'You're here for the season?'

His eyes lit up, and her blood fizzed. And there was *nothing* she could do about it. Dear God. She hadn't experienced this kind of *zing* since Connor.

And look how that had ended!

Grabbing a dishcloth, she wiped down the already spotless bar. 'I'm employed at Kings Reach for the next five months.'

The door at the back of the room opened and Fitz strode in. Tom straightened and did that sharpening-in-an-instant thing again. It was kind of hot, hinting as it did at an innate competence and an ability to focus that had her wondering if it would translate into other…areas.

Not that she had any intention of finding out.

Not even if he made a move? His eyes had lit up.

She slammed a lid on that thought. She wasn't getting hot and heavy with one of the King boys. Given what she thought of their father and what she hoped to do, that'd be… Well, it just didn't seem ethical.

Tom glanced at his daughter and then at Charlie, raised an eyebrow. She nodded. She'd keep an eye on Bea while he went and spoke to his brother. Rumours had been rife since the night of the ball. Apparently all was not well up at the big house.

Which could work in her favour. If Fraser was distracted it might make it easier to get inside his office.

She poured a beer for Fitz and then turned to Bea. 'Hey, Bea, you wanna learn a different way to fold serviettes—a prettier one? It's harder, though.'

Bea nodded and Tom dropped a kiss to her head before grabbing the beers and moving towards his brother. Charlie kept an eye on the two men as she demonstrated the new serviette fold to Bea. The other rec club patrons watched too.

The moment Fitz's gaze connected with Tom, she had the strangest feeling he'd like to turn tail and run. Instead, he took the beer Tom held out to him and they clinked glasses. They drank. When Tom finally spoke, something inside Fitz unhitched. She couldn't say why, but she was glad of it.

Fitz was a good guy. Worked hard. Had done great things with Hideaway Haven, his ecotourism business. She respected him. She *liked* him. Instinct told her Tom was cut from the same cloth. It'd be wrong for these two to fall out, to not get along. And it'd only add fuel to the currently rife rumour mill. These two men didn't deserve the kind of speculation currently doing the rounds. And neither did Bea.

Fraser, though…

She drummed her fingers on the bar. She needed to get inside his office. And every day counted. The sooner she had the contract, the sooner she could make Fraser do the honourable thing, and the sooner they could fix what needed fixing at Melaleuca.

They wouldn't have to sell the new stock at a devastating loss or spend all of their available funds feeding them, watching their resources dwindle away to nothing. Then Pop could stop worrying and working himself to the bone. Pop was in his seventies. If all of this stress made him ill…

Her stomach churned. *That* didn't bear thinking about.

Tom and Fitz spoke in low tones before straightening and moving towards the bar. Bea's face lit up when she saw her uncle. Just as suddenly, though, her smile became a scowl. 'You left!'

'Had an emergency I needed to sort out, Bea. But I'm back now and at your disposal. Why don't I show you how to play the pinball machine? And then I'll buy you dinner. It's shepherd's pie tonight—my favourite.'

Happy with that arrangement, Bea let Fitz help her down from her stool and lead her across to the other side of the room to the pinball machine. Tom straddled his stool again. 'I was getting a character reference.'

'Who for?' And then choked at his raised eyebrow. *'Me?'*

'I have a proposition for you, Charlie Ashwell of Melaleuca Downs.'

Those few short words conveyed a lot of information…and a lot of history. From what she could tell, the information reflected on her in a good way. 'All right, proposition away.' And then she laughed at how that sounded. 'This better be a business proposition, Tom King of Kings Reach.'

That crooked grin widened. 'Absolutely.' But

the wicked twinkle that briefly lit his eyes told her that he was imagining an altogether different kind of proposition. A more personal one. And that he liked whatever he saw in his mind's eye, and she couldn't help huffing out another laugh.

Folding her arms on the bar, she eyed him across its width. 'Okay, hit me with your *business* proposition.'

He sobered. 'There are a few things I need to sort out while I'm here at the station and I'm not sure how long it's going to take. Several weeks at least. Today proved I can't take care of my clients, oversee all of Bea's needs, *and* sort out what needs sorting out, all at the same time.'

She feigned shock. 'You mean you're *not* Superman?'

He didn't laugh as she'd meant him to. Instead he dragged a hand down his face. 'Today I've failed in every way it's possible to fail on the single-dad front. I...'

Whoa! This guy held himself to impossibly high standards. 'Hey, cut yourself some slack. The single-parent thing is a tough gig. Today was a rough day. They're going to happen. All you can do is weather the storm and move on.'

'Doesn't change the fact that I should've done better.'

Shadows flitted through his eyes and his lips twisted. He hadn't heard a word she'd said. 'Look at Bea now, Tom. She's having a ball. Tonight has been a good one from her perspective.'

'I guess.'

'You've saved something out of the turbulence. You ought to be proud of yourself, not beating yourself up.'

He stared at her for a moment. Slowly he straightened.

'You always beat up on yourself like this?'

He stretched his neck to the right and then the left. 'It's been a rough couple of days, that's all.' Clearly.

'But here's the thing, Charlie—I'm the kind of guy who learns from his mistakes. I've no intention of making the same mistakes tomorrow.'

She rolled her eyes. 'If you're anything like me, you'll make a whole new set instead.'

'I…' His jaw dropped as if her words left him speechless. And then he threw back his head and laughed. This man laughed with all of himself, and the laughter transformed him. Resting his head on his arms, his shoulders shaking, he gave himself up to it. She reached for the dishcloth and squeezed it tight. Oh, lordy lord. That laughter made Tom a hundred times more potently attractive.

He eventually lifted his head, his grin broad. 'You're the kind of person who keeps a body grounded, right?'

She stuck her nose in the air. 'I resent being likened to an earthing rod.'

Grey eyes twinkled. 'You're perfect.'

She crossed arms over a thumping heart. 'For?'

'I need help with Bea. I need someone to oversee her School of the Air lessons, to supervise her when I'm in meetings, to keep her occupied.'

Her?

'Both Bea and Fitz think you're fabulous.'

Fitz had said that?

'So, Charlie Ashwell of Melaleuca Downs, waitress, barmaid, and stockwoman extraordinaire, are you interested in adding nanny to the list of your many accomplishments?'

He wanted *her* to be Bea's nanny? She'd love it! What fun. They'd—

Her excitement sank beneath a dank wave of reality. She pressed a hand to her stomach. She couldn't. No matter how much she wanted to.

Tom had no idea what she was up to, and she couldn't see him being thrilled about it if he did. Or offering her this job. If she accepted, she'd be taking advantage of him. She'd be taking advantage of Fitz too.

The word *advantage*, though, caught at her. Tom and Fitz had been blessed with advantages she'd only ever dreamed of. They'd lived lives of privilege that were beyond her scope of understanding.

Pop's face rose in her mind. He was the true victim here.

She wasn't trying to defraud Tom. If she took the position as Bea's nanny, she'd do it to the best of her ability. Bea wouldn't lack for anything. Beneath the bar, she twisted the dishcloth in her hands. She wasn't trying to defraud Fraser either. She just wanted him to do *the right thing*.

She moistened suddenly dry lips. She might be stepping into morally grey territory, but she wasn't trying to hurt anyone. 'I have some questions,' she heard herself say.

'I'd be disappointed if you didn't,' Tom said, surprised at how much he wanted Charlie to say yes.

Bea adored her—with reason. Everything Charlie did seemed easy and natural; fun. She threw herself into everything, from waitressing and being a barmaid to chatting to a five-year-old and giving her a task that made her feel important, with gusto. Beneath the twinkling good humour was a quiet authority. This was a woman who had boundaries that she'd hold firm to.

Easing back on his stool, he tried to work out what it was about her that had captured his attention. Charlie lacked impatience, and she lacked urgency. She did what needed doing, without fanfare or calling attention to it, and simply enjoyed the ride. Competent was the word that sprang to mind. Low-key and competent. And he found himself drawn to it.

Since his father's announcement on Saturday night, he'd felt agitated and impatient. Everything had felt urgent. But half an hour in this woman's company had him relaxing, taking a deep breath…and feeling not so isolated.

Charlie gazed up at the ceiling now and chewed

on a rather voluptuous bottom lip. He stared at that mouth and something deep and dormant inside him lifted its head and stretched...

He dragged his gaze away. *That* was the last thing he needed. He wasn't starting something with any woman. He suppressed a shudder. He wouldn't be here long enough to let anything beyond a working relationship develop.

If she agrees to this job, she'll practically become part of the family for the duration. There'll be ample opportunity for things to develop.

Not going to happen.

He went to sip his beer, but he'd finished it so he grabbed his water instead. 'Come on, Charlie, hit me with your questions.' The sooner he eased her concerns, the sooner he could have her on board and the sooner he could rest easy about Bea.

Charlie straightened. 'I brought my horses and my team of dogs with me.'

He'd figured as much when she'd said she was working at the station for the season, and Fitz had confirmed it. 'They can remain where they are and you'll have a chance to exercise them every day.' He'd need to work that into his schedule somehow.

'Okay, excellent.'

She took her responsibilities seriously, which was a tick in her favour. He waited for her to ask the question he'd expected her to have led with—

what was the remuneration? It was the question he'd have asked first.

'Where would I sleep?'

Dammit. 'Ask me about the pay, Charlie.'

Her eyes narrowed. 'We're going through *my* hierarchy of questions, Tom, not yours. And if this is some kind of test to see if I can hold my own then I'm going to pass it with flying colours.'

Strength of character was all well and good, but it could lead to problems too—the kind that might have him drawing a big black line through her name. 'Before we go any further I've a question for you, and it could be a deal-breaker depending on your answer.'

She folded her arms and stuck out her hip. 'Okay.'

'The directions I give you about Bea…'

Something inside her unhitched. 'Will be followed to the letter even if I don't agree with them. If you don't want me to take her down to the waterhole, I won't. If you don't want her eating red frogs, she won't eat red frogs. If you don't want her left alone with—'

She broke off, her cheeks turning an interesting shade of pink. 'She's *your* daughter, Tom. Those are your decisions to make, not mine.'

'What were you going to say?'

Her gaze slid away from his. 'I was just searching for examples and…'

'Finish what you were going to say.'

Huffing out a breath, she met his gaze squarely.

'I was going to say that if you didn't want her left alone with anyone in particular then I'll make sure she isn't left alone with that person.'

'You were going to say Fraser.'

She hesitated and then nodded.

His stomach went as hard and cold as a stone buried six feet beneath dark, dank earth. 'Any reason you'd think Bea shouldn't be left alone with him?'

'None whatsoever.' The promptness of her reply had the cold receding. 'Other than it's a well-known fact that the two of you have a…tempestuous relationship.'

That was one way of putting it.

'Along with the fact that the rumour mill hasn't stopped speculating since Saturday night.'

'Speculating?'

'Jack's and Logan's hasty departures were noted.'

Dammit. They *had* to keep this out of the papers.

'All I'm saying is that whatever you say in regards to Bea goes. End of story.'

He nodded. He should never have doubted her.

'Now back to *my* questions, Tom. Where would I sleep?'

He'd be dragging her away from the independence and fun of hanging out in the staff quarters, no doubt with her friends. Did she have a boyfriend here? Why hadn't he thought to ask

Fitz? How would she feel being stuck up at the homestead instead?

'I'd need you to stay up at the house. Bea rises early and I sometimes have an early morning meeting with a client.'

'I see.'

It didn't look as if that was a problem. 'Bea and I are staying in one of the guest suites. I've an en-suite bedroom and next to that is Bea's room. You can have the bedroom on the other side of hers. Across the hall is the bathroom, and there's a pleasant sitting area that leads out to a balcony.' He shrugged. 'It's nice.' It was.

Her smile made his skin tighten. 'Bigger than the rooms in the staff quarters, then.'

'Absolutely.' But minus the camaraderie.

She gave a funny grimace. 'Will anyone be upset—rake me over the coals—if I ever slip down to the kitchen for a midnight snack or to make a hot drink?'

What an odd question. 'Of course not.'

Her gaze slid away and one slim shoulder lifted. 'It's hard to feel at home in someone else's house. I wouldn't want to step on anyone's toes. It's good to know the rules.'

'Ah, house rules. Hmm… Mrs Mac is pretty particular, so I wouldn't leave the kitchen in a mess.'

'Hell no.'

'Don't play your music too loud. Don't run. Don't kick footballs in the house. Don't play cricket in the house. No rough-housing. Don't speak with your mouth full.'

She laughed as he rattled off his list. 'Same at my house. I should manage just fine, then.'

He wished he'd asked Fitz more about her and her family.

Later.

'Okay.' She pressed her hands together.

Ask about the money.

She glanced at him from beneath her eyelashes and winced. He automatically straightened. 'What?' He sounded defensive, but he couldn't help it.

'You'll have noticed I like to laugh and tease people—have fun, share a joke.'

Something Bea responded to. 'And?'

'Some people—some *men*,' she clarified, 'read more into that than they should.'

She was warning him off?

'I don't want there to be any of misunderstandings. I'm not interested in that kind of fun, Tom, and—'

'*Stop!*' He held up both hands. 'Don't say another word. I agree. Totally.' And to think he'd thought he might have to subtly signal to her that he wasn't interested in anything like that. 'You won't have to run that particular gauntlet with me. I swear.'

Blue eyes raked his face. 'I hope I haven't offended you. I just find it's better to be upfront about these things.'

'Totally! Ours is going to be a business relationship only—if you say yes, that is. And because you've yet to ask, let me outline the remuneration package. Perry,' the station manager, 'will have to employ someone else to do the job he's originally employed you for, and I don't know how long I'm going to need you. So I'll cover your entire wage for the next five months. I'm not going to be here anywhere near that length of time, but it wouldn't be fair to leave you short.'

She stared at him. 'How long do you expect to be here?'

'Hopefully no longer than three weeks.'

She shook her head as if she hadn't heard him correctly.

'Fitz indicated that if Perry could find work for you when Bea and I leave, that he'll re-employ you. Fitz seemed to think there was a ninety-nine per cent chance of that happening. He said you were too good to let go.'

'He said that?'

'Yep.'

'God, I *love* your brother.'

He froze. 'You *love* him?'

'In a platonic, he's-a-great-guy-and-a-good-friend kind of way.'

He let out a breath. Thank God for that. The thought of Charlie and Fitz together was somehow wrong.

'So in effect, I have a chance of doubling my money this season?'

'Yep.'

She stuck out a hand. 'You have yourself a deal.'

He closed his hand around hers. 'Thank you.' He didn't release it immediately. 'The waterhole is fine, but not too many red frogs, please.'

'Roger.' She hesitated. 'And Fraser?'

A bad taste stretched through his mouth. 'Supervised, please.' He was ninety per cent certain that Fraser wouldn't do anything to hurt Bea, but Fraser had a temper and it had led to disaster once before.

That's not fair.

Maybe not. But it was Tom's job to protect Bea and a ten per cent risk was more than he was prepared to take.

Charlie didn't say anything, just nodded. The heat from her hand had started to filter into his blood. He reluctantly released it.

'So how's this for a plan?' Charlie slouched down on the bar again. 'I come over after breakfast. I'll supervise Bea's School of the Air lessons. And after that she can help me pack and settle in?'

'Sounds perfect.'

It meant tomorrow he could confront Fraser.

CHAPTER THREE

'WOULD YOU LIKE a rundown on Day One of Bea and Charlie's Most Excellent Adventures?' Charlie plonked herself down on the sofa in the sitting room of Tom and Bea's suite of rooms and only just prevented herself from lifting her feet to the coffee table. *Manners, Charlie.*

The suite had dark-panelled walls and ornate plasterwork ceilings. A thick Persian rug that probably cost the price of a small sheep station softened the dark floorboards of the sitting room. Instead of priceless vases and ornaments, though, there was a doll of Bea's resting on the coffee table alongside a book about fairies, and a jumper of Tom's that had been thrown on the back of an armchair. The chairs and furniture were antiques and of the finest quality, and a Margaret Olley still life hung on the wall. The nonchalant opulence of it all blew her mind.

Tom glanced up from his leather armchair and Charlie did her best not to wince. He didn't look any better rested than when he'd ambled into the rec club last night. 'Is everything okay?'

Tired or not, his lips still twitched into a smile. The creases around his mouth deepened, and she fought a swoon. Like her, he wore jeans and a T-shirt—his in the palest of blues that highlighted the grey of his eyes. She fought a frown. *And* the grey tinge to his face.

'I believe I've already had a blow-by-blow run-down of your excellent and epic adventures—and when I say blow-by-blow, believe me, I mean microscopically detailed.'

Charlie bit back a grin. Bea could talk the ears off a donkey. 'She's a fun kid, Tom.'

His eyes twinkled and some of his colour returned. 'If non-stop motion and non-stop questions are your idea of fun.'

She feigned shock. 'You mean they're not everyone's?'

His low chuckle raised all of the fine hairs on her arms. It had her imagining things she shouldn't be imagining.

Go to bed, Charlie. Now.

'What were you like, Charlie, as a five-year-old?'

'Oh, I was full of beans,' she said. 'But the adults around me were always busy. You know what station life is like. Melaleuca resources never stretched to a nanny. So I had to ask my questions carefully when Mum, Pop, Nan or Uncle Wayne had time to answer them.'

'You learned to be self-reliant early on?'

'Not sure self-reliant is the right term.' She

curled her legs beneath her. 'I did learn to entertain myself, though.'

'No siblings?'

'Not a single one.' Unlike him. She kept her voice upbeat, but caught a flash of sympathy in his eyes. 'I did, however, have an entire raft of imaginary friends.'

He settled back with a grin.

'And I'll let you into a little secret. I sometimes still chat to them when I'm out in the middle of the Never-Never under a wide blue sky.'

'I have it on good authority you're never alone in the middle of the Never-Never. That you have Cranky Frank and Lady Trippy Fast Feet, along with Good Miss Molly and the rest of the crew to keep you company.' His brow pleated. 'Did I get that right?'

She had to laugh. She'd be lost without Frank and Lady—her horses—and Molly and the rest of her team of kelpies. 'Word perfect,' she assured him. 'They're my best friends in the whole wide world.'

Okay, things were in danger of becoming too cosy, and she'd promised herself she wouldn't let that happen. She might no longer be that silly teenager who believed in soulmates, but she'd be foolish to ignore the zip and zing between her and Tom. She didn't need the distraction and neither did he. She started to rise.

'I'm sorry if you'd rather be out there under a wide blue sky rather than stuck indoors, Charlie.'

She lowered herself back to the sofa, bit her lip. Why was he apologising to her? 'Bea and I will be spending a lot of time under that wide blue sky, Tom. I'm not missing out.'

'We both know it's not the same as being on muster. Being a nanny wasn't what you'd planned for.'

A multitude of tiny knives stabbed her. She had to remind herself of all the advantages he'd grown up with, of his privilege. 'You made me an offer that I accepted of my own free will. End of story. Bea and I are going to have a great time.'

Her words didn't seem to lighten his load one little bit.

'If you're only going to be at Kings Reach for three weeks, Tom, it's not fair you pay me five months' salary. Especially if Perry finds work for me afterwards.'

A weight settled on her shoulders. She swallowed and reminded herself that she wasn't taking advantage of Tom—not in the same way Fraser had taken advantage of Pop. *She'd* do the job he was paying her for. *She'd* keep her side of the bargain. Unlike Fraser.

'What wouldn't be fair is for you to miss out on contracted work because you were kind enough to help me out.'

Oh, God! She fought an urge to confess all immediately.

'And the way it's going, I could be here for longer than anticipated anyway.'

The prospect clearly didn't please him. 'In that case it's just as well I'm going to thoroughly enjoy my stint as Bea's nanny.' She could at least ease that concern from his mind. She had no intention of being another thing he worried about. Where she could, she'd ease his worry. It was the least she could do.

He rose. 'You're something else, Charlie Ashwell. Thank you for your enthusiasm.' Grey eyes assessed her. 'You wouldn't be interested in coming to the city, would you?'

'Not even for double the money. Not even for the money times ten.' She rose too, which brought them a tiny bit closer. It shouldn't have made any difference, but the faint tang of his scent—citrus and juniper—tantalised her senses and she pulled a deep breath of it into her lungs. His gaze lowered to her lips and her heart stuttered and her pulse leapt. She took a tiny step back, gave a shaky smile. 'Not even for the crown jewels.'

His lips twitched. 'So that's a no, then?'

She wanted to pat the spot above her heart and tell it to slow down. 'I'm a country girl through and through. There's nowhere else I'd rather be.'

He raised an eyebrow—non-judgy, easy and assessing all at once. It was kind of—

It's not sexy!

'I felt that way once.'

But something had changed. He'd become a

city boy. And she trusted city boys about as far as she could kick them. She edged away. 'Night, Tom.'

'Night, Charlie.'

After lunch the following day, Charlie took Bea through the finer points of hopscotch, which was when Tom came stomping across from the direction of the rec club, a scowl plastered across his face. 'Hiya, Tom,' she called out before Bea caught sight of him and his dark expression.

The scowl cleared as if by magic. 'Hello, ladies.'

'We're playing hopscotch, Daddy!' Bea raced over, stared up at him, hands on her hips. 'Charlie is the champion of the whole wide Kimberley and she says she won't let me beat her. That she has—' She glanced at Charlie.

'A reputation to maintain,' Charlie supplied.

'But I *want* to win!'

He lifted his little girl into his arms with a swoony ease, and Charlie rolled her eyes. Not everything Tom did was swoony.

You sure about that?

'You wouldn't want Charlie to cheat to let you win, would you?'

Bea didn't look convinced and Charlie had to bite back a laugh.

'But I *really* want to beat her.' Bea pouted.

'Then you have to practise hard and beat her fair and square.' He let her slide back to the ground and Charlie refused to imagine for a single solitary second what that might feel like. 'And then if you do beat her, it'll be a real win.'

Charlie stuck out a hip, blew on her fingernails and pretend to polish them on her shirt. 'You want to have a shot at the trophy, hotshot?'

He grinned, but those intriguing grey eyes caught on her hip. His mouth opened, but no words emerged. His Adam's apple bobbed. Coughing, he backed up a step. 'Tempting as that offer is, I have…work.' Pointing towards the homestead, he fled.

She stared after him.

Bea tugged on her hand. 'Ready?'

'Absolutely!' She swung back. 'Let's do this.'

That night, when the house was dark and silent, Charlie tiptoed down the stairs, but halted halfway. A light filtered out from beneath Fraser's office door.

Damn. He was working?

She silently turned and headed back up the stairs. Maybe she'd have better luck tomorrow night.

'Okay, let's make sure we have everything.' It was the following afternoon and Charlie plonked herself down on the stairs and opened her backpack. Bea perched beside her. 'We have paints and paintbrushes, crayons, colour pencils and sketchpads. Any other drawing bits and bobs you want, Honey Bea?'

Bea shook her head. 'I have my hat.' She reached up to touch it.

Sun safety had been one of the School of the Air topics today. 'Me too.' She took an inventory of their other supplies—blanket, water bottles, snacks from Mrs McRae. Right, all they needed now was their boots—

The door to their right flew open. 'I don't have time for this right now!'

Fraser stormed out of his office, Tom hot on his heels.

'Then when?'

'If it's so damn important, make an appointment with Annalise!'

Her jaw dropped. Had Fraser seriously just told his son that if he wanted to speak with him to make an appointment with his PA? She tried to imagine Mum or Pop telling her to do that and couldn't.

'I'm leaving for Sydney in the morning.'

She winced at the way the muscles in Tom's jaw clenched. 'How long will you be gone?'

'No idea.'

'Helpful,' Tom drawled. 'And convenient.'

'Look, I—'

Charlie cleared her throat and stood. Both men swung to stare. 'Bea and I are heading down to the waterhole, aren't we, Bea?'

Bea pressed against Charlie's side. She eyed her grandfather as if he might be an ogre.

'Well, we'll just grab our boots and...'

Fraser stalked off.

Tom didn't follow.

Charlie wrinkled her nose. 'Sorry if we interrupted. We just…' She waved at the stairs and her backpack.

Tom's grey eyes swirled with a mix of emotions while the tight set of his shoulders told their own story. 'Why don't you come with us?' she said on impulse. It might help him unwind. 'We decided the sun and the blue sky and the chance to breathe in the fresh air shouldn't be wasted.'

'We're going to paint Charlie's favourite beetle. I'll even let you use my favourite paintbrush.' Bea sat on the bench to pull on the boots Charlie handed her.

'And,' Charlie pointed at him, before leaning against the door frame of the boot room and pulling on her boots, 'we have lamingtons that Mrs McRae made fresh this morning.'

'I…' He stared in the direction Fraser had disappeared.

'With jam and cream,' she added, waggling her eyebrows.

He started to laugh. 'Best offer I've had all day.'

Tom hadn't realised how frustrating his stay at Kings Reach would prove to be. Fraser had been impossible to pin down. First there'd been the hangers-on after the ball, who'd all finally left, thank God. Then between his own meetings and

Fraser's, and his responsibilities to Bea, and Fraser's gallivanting around the station…

Gallivanting isn't fair.

It was as if Fraser was doing it to avoid him. And now Fraser was going to Sydney. To see his lawyers? Had Tom ever felt more useless in his life?

Sure you have.

The thought made him flinch.

He pulled himself back into straight lines. First things first. He'd go down to the waterhole with his little girl, and cool down. Experience had taught him long ago that approaching Fraser when he was tense never ended well.

Oh, and approaching him when you're relaxed always ends in pots of gold at the end of rainbows? Damn it, he was the wrong son for the job! Logan had his logic and lawyerly tactics, Fitz was the one who'd returned and brought with him a new and successful vision for Kings Reach, while Jack had always been the golden son.

All Tom had brought was discord and disrespect. And that was a direct quote. Had his father taken an instant dislike to him at birth—or had it grown slowly over time? He'd been fourteen when he'd heard overheard Fraser tell Eliza, 'We're going to have to find Tom a job away from the station.'

That day he'd fallen off his horse. His father had picked him up and dusted him off and asked what had happened. Tom had explained that he'd been trying to calculate the number of cockatoos that could fit on Kings Reach land based on the number in the flock that had just passed overhead—he'd done a rough count of their number—and had then multiplied it by the number of hectares they had.

Fraser had frowned. 'How is this useful?'

'Not useful. Not realistic either.' He'd known how ecosystems worked. If one element was out it threw the entire system out. That number of cockatoos on Kings Reach would be a disaster. 'But it's fun to work it out all the same.'

Fraser had shaken his head and tossed Tom back in the saddle. 'Pay attention when you're on your horse, Tom.' His hand had been heavy on Tom's thigh as if to drive his point home. 'We're a long way from a doctor if you break an arm or something worse.'

That advice had been useful. He'd heeded it. It wasn't until he'd overheard Fraser's words that night, though, that he'd felt as if he'd let his father down in some inexplicable way—had failed some test he hadn't been aware he'd been taking. That he'd been found wanting. That Fraser hadn't seen a future for Tom at Kings Reach. That was the real start of his issues with his father. *Not* Will's death.

A bump to his hip unbalanced him and brought him crashing back to the present moment. 'Earth to Tom.'

He blinked down at the eyes that danced up

into his. Charlie handed him the backpack, which he automatically took, before opening the front door and ushering him and Bea outside.

'I was tempted to break into that David Bowie song—the one about Major Tom and Ground Control. My mum loves that song. So does my Pop.'

Bea bounced between them. 'Sing it, Charlie… Please,' she added when Tom shot her a pointed look.

Charlie launched into the song immediately and he found himself grinning at her enthusiasm and the sheer gusto with which she attacked it. She had a nice voice, could hold a tune, and he found himself joining in. Bea danced, clapping her hands. Charlie made boom-boom noises to signify drums, so he played air guitar, and by the time they made it down to the waterhole they were all laughing—were floppy with it—and he collapsed onto the picnic blanket that Charlie spread out, wondering how on earth he could feel like this when a minute ago he'd been so wrung out.

Lying back, he closed his eyes and relished the warmth of the sun on his face.

'Don't go to sleep, Daddy! We—'

'No, no, don't move,' Charlie countered. 'Bea, we can draw your daddy as a warm-up.'

And just like that Charlie gifted him a moment's reprieve—a tiny pocket of peace. Dragging in a breath, he identified the camphor-like scent of a nearby snappy gum on a breeze already softened by the scent of kapok flowers. The melodic chirping of a fairy wren rippled through the air along with the distinctive cry of a black cockatoo. The stream that fed the waterhole burbled and splashed over rocks and the ground beneath his back felt both soft and solid. For a moment it felt like heaven—as if he was exactly where he ought to be.

And he couldn't remember the last time he'd felt like that.

'No frowning,' Charlie ordered.

He smoothed out his face, but immediately became aware of other things—Charlie's unique vanilla and eucalyptus scent, the sound of a pencil moving across paper… He fancied he could feel her gaze roving over his face and down the length of his body. Did she like what she saw? If he opened his eyes would he spy desire there?

He wanted to. The acknowledgement had things inside him clenching. Since Madeline's death, he'd neglected that side of his life. He was a single father—Bea had to come first. *Doesn't mean you have to be a goddamn monk.*

Maybe not, but now wasn't the time or the place. And his daughter's nanny definitely wasn't the right person.

So stop thinking about it.

'When can I open my eyes?'

'Whenever you want to.'

The smile in her voice had him smiling too,

and it was the darnedest thing. The sky above was a crisp blue and the grey-green of the coolabah trees rustled as a breeze danced through them. He turned his head to meet eyes every bit as blue as the sky, and rose up onto his elbows.

Charlie brushed a hand across her face. 'What?'

'You've been nothing but cheerful and good-natured since I met you.'

'That's because, as I believe I've told you before, I'm a woman of action, not a cowpat.' One shoulder lifted. 'Besides, you met me on Saturday night and it's only Wednesday. There's time yet for me to blot my copybook.'

'What gets you het up?'

She started. 'Het up? I...' Her cheeks turned an intriguing shade of pink as her gaze slid away and he had to fight a grin because he knew she was thinking wicked thoughts. Illicit thoughts. He wanted to thrust an arm in the air. Charlie Ashwell saw him as a man—not just as Bea's dad, and not just a King from Kings Reach. But as a hot-blooded man she found attractive.

His gaze moved beyond her to where Bea lay fast asleep, her cheek resting on her sketchpad. A blob of blue—was that him?—marked the page. Staring at that blob, he let out a long breath. He couldn't do anything wicked or illicit with Charlie, no matter how much the thought tempted him.

He sat up, scratched a hand through his hair. 'What makes you angry, Charlie?' He focused on redirecting both of their thoughts.

'Injustice, broken promises—people who don't keep their word.'

Who'd broken promises they'd made her?

'Cruelty. I don't like people being mean. And if you really want to see me angry, mistreat an animal.'

'I don't want to see you angry. I don't like any of those things either.'

Her eyes turned assessing. 'What makes you angry?'

'My father.'

The words left him before he thought better of saying them. Charlie didn't laugh. She stared back, a frown in her eyes. 'Is everything okay, Tom?'

He ought to brush it off. He knew—thanks to her—that speculation was rife on the station, that people thought something had happened at the ball; something big and scandalous. And they were right. But he and his brothers sure as heck didn't want that story breaking. Charlie, though, was looking after his little girl. He needed her to act as a buffer between Bea and any potential scandal.

'There's some family stuff happening, but I'm trying to sort it out. And Fraser is being…'

'Difficult?'

'Not only can I *not* pin him down, even if I could I doubt I could make him listen.'

'I don't believe that for a moment. I think you can do anything you set your mind to.'

He sent her one of *those* looks that he reserved for Bea. 'You don't even know me.'

'I know you've created a fabulously successful business. You're a brilliant dad. And Fitz thinks you're the best thing since sliced bread.'

He stared. *He did?*

She leaned towards him and the scent of vanilla and eucalyptus wrapped around him like a hug. 'Play to your strengths. What are you good at?'

'Facts and figures. Projections and calculations. I...' He froze. *Making money.* 'You—' he pointed '—are a genius.'

She shrugged as if to say, of course I am. It made him laugh, but...

What are you good at? He was good at making money and calculating risk.

If he presented Fraser with the likely costs of a lawsuit, and the lack of gain his actions would have on the station—the financial damage it'd do—all backed up by hard facts and figures... Fraser might not care about the emotional damage he did, but he'd always cared about money. Out here money meant security and prosperity. Money had always ensured the station's survival during the hard times.

And money gave a person power. Fraser cared about the King name. The four generations of outback Kings before him had all received knighthoods or been awarded Orders of Australia. Fraser probably hadn't given up hopes of receiving one himself. But if he lost a bucketload of money in a dead-end court case that dragged the family name through the mud…

Reaching over, he gripped Charlie's hand. 'A genius,' he repeated.

He'd had to lean across, balancing on one elbow to reach her, and the momentum of his seizing her hand pulled her towards him until she too rested on her elbow. It drew their faces close together.

The blue of her irises deepened, her pupils dilating. Her lips parted as if in shock, or to draw much-needed air into cramped lungs. Charlie had lips shaped like the plump curves of a cello. He'd never been musical and he had no idea what made him think of cellos now except… There was something melodic about the way this woman approached life—a gusto and grace, an odd combination of energy and elegance that threw him off balance. Instinct told him that kissing her would be something else.

It'd be so easy to breach the distance and press his lips to hers, to entice them into a slow, sensual dance. Charlie's gaze roved over his face and the blood in his veins pounded. She bit her lip before moistening it. The pulse in her throat raced, longing flickered across her face. His nerves stretched taut. Maybe she'd kiss him first?

She gave a slumbrous blink. His mouth went bone-dry. Her chin lifted a fraction, angling her lips in an unconscious invitation. *Yes!* He—

Charlie jerked free, throwing off his hand,

and he almost face-planted into the blanket. She moved away from him. Far away. As in off the blanket. She perched on a boulder overlooking the waterhole.

Smothering a groan, he rolled onto his back before forcing himself to his feet and moving to where she sat. He didn't get too close, though. He didn't want to crowd her. 'I'm sorry, Charlie. That was utterly out of order. I'm your employer, for God's sake, and—'

'Oh, hush, Tom.' She grimaced. 'I'm just as much to blame…for that—' she glanced at the blanket '—as you. I just don't think it's a very good idea.'

His hands clenched. Not a good idea at all. He had a habit of searching for distraction during times when emotions ran high. And they didn't get much higher than right now at Kings Reach. He would *not* make the same mistake with Charlie that he had with Madeline. 'Agreed.'

'You obviously have a lot going on at the moment. Plus…'

He raised an eyebrow.

'You're a city boy and I'm a country girl. And while opposites attract, blah blah.'

He smiled at her shorthand.

'They don't live happily ever after.'

As his marriage had proven. The reminder froze his bone marrow to ice.

'And maybe neither of us is looking for a happy-ever-after, but, given the situation—the fact I'm looking after your daughter—it'd be best just to…'

'Not cross that particular line,' he finished for her.

She nodded.

Behind them a helicopter took off from the airfield, the blades slashing the air, and Tom swung towards the sound. Had Fraser left this afternoon instead of going tomorrow? He bit back a whole rash of curses he couldn't utter in the presence of a lady…and certainly not in front of his daughter. 'Coward,' he muttered, glaring as it lifted into the air.

He turned to Charlie. 'I ought to get back to work. You and Bea enjoy the rest of your afternoon.' He strode off in the direction of the homestead. And just like his father on Saturday night, he didn't look back.

CHAPTER FOUR

THE TINIEST SLIVER of light from the quarter-moon lit Charlie's bedroom. Slipping out of bed, she pulled on a thick pair of woollen socks and dragged on her dressing gown—a fluffy number in a combat-fatigue print that the boys had bought for her birthday. It still made them grin whenever she wore it. When she was home, that was.

Home. An ache stretched through her. What she wouldn't give to be there now.

She cut the thought dead; tied the sash of her robe tight. Once she'd made Fraser do the right thing, and worked at topping up Melaleuca's coffers, she could go home then.

Right. She checked off her mental list. Socks for silence—tick; robe for modesty—tick; loins girded—tick. The sooner she found the contract and made a copy, the sooner she could confront Fraser, and the sooner she could make things right.

If you get caught, you'll be fired, and you'll lose a whole season's worth of wages.

A cramp pulled her chest out of shape. She

didn't want to imagine the look on Tom's face if that happened. Maybe she should put this off for a few weeks.

What the hell…? *No!* Every day counted. Plus Fraser had left the building. He wouldn't be working late. He wouldn't be here to catch her. She hated the thought of disappointing Tom and Fitz. But she hated the thought of Pop being taken advantage of more.

So don't get caught.

They'd call that Plan A. Hopefully she could get in and out in no time at all. She'd positively visualised this entire scenario. There'd be a filing cabinet in the office—probably several—and she just needed to find the one with A for Ashwell or possibly M for Melaleuca Downs, grab the contract, and get the hell out of Dodge. Simple.

Charlie had to pass both Bea's and Tom's bedrooms. *Don't imagine what Tom wears to bed. Don't imagine kissing Tom.* Just…*don't.*

She couldn't let anything happen between them. She was *lying* to him. If he found out what she was up to… Her stomach shrivelled to the size of a hard, dry walnut. It didn't bear thinking about. But to lie and then kiss him? That'd be unforgivable.

She carefully stepped over the floorboard that squeaked. When she reached the stairs she stepped over the fourth one down that creaked, though she was probably far enough away from

Tom's room for him not to hear it. Except he was a parent, and parents had supersonic hearing.

At the bottom of the stairs she halted and listened. Nothing. Not a peep. It was after midnight and everyone should be tucked up tight in their beds. The strip beneath Fraser's office door was reassuringly dark. Slipping across the foyer, she reached for the old-fashioned doorknob, her fingers curling around the cold brass. She turned the knob and...

Nothing.

She tried again with both hands. Same result. She blinked in the semi-darkness. Dammit all to damnation, the door was locked! She hadn't positively visualised that particular scenario, hadn't factored it into the equation at all.

Some cat burglar she proved to be.

Positively visualise a solution.

Reaching up on tiptoe, she felt along the top of the doorframe—nothing. Next she moved to the antique dresser that stood to one side of the door. As quietly as she could she opened the drawers one by one. All of them were empty. If this was at Melaleuca Downs it'd be full of cricket balls, maps, lengths of twine, dog leads...sunscreen.

Resting her hands on her hips, she took a step back and surveyed the dresser. It was old—a proper antique. She'd bet it had a secret compartment like the ones she'd seen in those old movies her Nan liked to watch. When all seemed lost they always provided a vital clue. She pressed a tiny carved rose, a whole row of them parading along the front edge, but nothing happened. There was an assortment of other adornments and do-dahs. Gah! She could be here till morning.

She twisted one of the drawer knobs—first left and then right—but no click sounded, no drawer sprang free. She tried another rose and then another. It couldn't be that hard—

'What are you doing?'

She gave a muffled scream and swung around to find Tom peering over the stairs, a frown in his eyes as he muffled a yawn. Thank God she hadn't been holding anything or she'd have dropped it and woken the entire household.

'Do you have a fetish for antique furniture or something?'

She pulled her robe around her more securely. 'Funny you should say that—*no*.'

He grinned and if anything her heart rate only increased.

She gestured at the dresser. 'It is beautiful, though. It made me think of an old movie—'

'The one with the dresser that has a secret compartment?'

She feigned shock, even as a laugh bubbled up inside her. 'You've seen it too?'

He ambled down the stairs with the lazy grace of a big cat, and her heart went bumpity-bump with his every step. Reaching across, he touched something on the side of the dresser. A secret compartment immediately popped open.

Her jaw dropped. 'No way!' Peeking inside, she blew out a breath. Empty. 'Where's the locket or the journal or the key to the mysterious cabin in the woods?'

His low chuckle had all the fine hairs on her arms lifting. 'There's another secret compartment. If you find it, I'll give you a prize.'

She crushed the rather intriguing images that rose in her mind under a figurative heel—a hard one. Pushing the secret compartment back into place, she found the same spot Tom had pressed and opened it again. 'A prize?'

'I'll make you the best ice-cream sundae you've ever had in your life.'

She grinned.

'And if you can't find it then you have to bake me your favourite cake.'

Tom had a sweet tooth? 'That would be a lemon drizzle cake. Delicious with or without whipped cream. Either way, looks like we're going to have a party.' She pushed the secret compartment back into place and gestured. 'Empty.'

'I thought we'd already established that.'

'Not the compartment.' She led him in the direction of the kitchen because she needed some pretext for being up at this time of night. 'The dresser itself.'

He leaned a hip against the bench and watched her pour milk into two mugs and pop them in the microwave. 'So you're nosy by nature?'

She stuck said nose in the air. 'I prefer the

term *curious*. If that dresser was at Melaleuca it'd be chock full of assorted bits and bobs. And as it's located in a public thoroughfare, I figured it wouldn't hold anything personal. So I had a peek thinking I might find something fun for Bea and me.'

'Like what?'

She shrugged. 'Something you boys might've played with when you were kids. Skittles, quoits, a fire engine, toy soldiers, a plastic cricket bat—' she retrieved the mugs and reached for the jar of hot chocolate '—an abandoned craft project we could've rescued, yo-yos, a game of Twister—'

'Okay, okay, I get the picture.'

His grin held far too much power, and when he aimed it at her it sent an electric charge zapping through her, which had her inadvertently scattering powdered chocolate across the countertop.

Reaching across, he collected some on the end of his finger and popped it in his mouth. She watched the way his lips closed about his finger and an ache sprang to life at the very centre of her, as if just like the dresser she too had a secret compartment he'd magically unlocked. Heat slid along her veins and an ache bloomed to life between her thighs.

Tom glanced across and froze in the act of reaching for more of the spilled chocolate. Something in his eyes flared, as if he'd like to lick her in the same way he just had that chocolate. Her knees trembled and—

Tom snapped away. 'I'll grab the marshmallows while you clean that up.'

Gritting her teeth, she reached for the kitchen sponge and rubbed the chocolate away for all she was worth. She needed to pull herself back into straight lines. She didn't want to imagine what it would be like to kiss Tom, to make love with Tom. That could never happen. She straightened. She *wasn't* handing her heart to another city boy who had plans to sail off into the sunset without her.

Tom placed three marshmallows in each mug in an identical configuration. She pointed. 'Now, that's a big tick in your favour.' Seizing her mug, she moved across to the table and prayed her composure would hold.

'Bea has educated me in the finer points of marshmallow distribution—not just the number, but also the placement.' He hooked out the seat opposite. 'Woe betide anyone who gets it wrong.'

'I'll keep that in mind.' She kept her gaze studiously averted and turned her mind to her latest problem instead. Who would have a key to Fraser's office? Fraser himself and Annalise of course. English rose Annalise had been working at Kings Reach as Fraser's PA for two years now, but she was far too vigilant to leave her keys lying around for anyone to pick up. What about Mrs McRae—would the housekeeper have one? Maybe Fitz? How on earth was Charlie going to get her hands on one of them?

Tom reached over to tweak the lapel of her robe. 'Combat fatigues, huh?'

She refused to consider how closely his fingers had just come to brushing against her breast. 'A birthday present from the boys.'

'The boys?'

'My cousins. My mum's little brother is significantly younger than her, and they're significantly younger than me. The oldest will finish high school this year.'

'Wayne's kids?'

'You know Wayne?'

'Only by sight. He's older than me and my brothers. Is he managing Melaleuca now?'

Okay, wow. 'You've really fallen off the gossip mill, huh?'

He frowned. 'What have I missed?'

'Wayne had an accident. It'd be twelve years ago now. Overturned his quad bike. Broke his back. He's in a wheelchair—paralysed from the waist down.'

Tom sagged. 'Hell, Charlie. I didn't know. I'm sorry.'

She shrugged. 'I'll tell him you said hello.'

Tom recognised the shadows in the blue of Charlie's eyes, but she blinked them away, refusing to let them settle. She wasn't the kind of person to dwell on her or her family's misfortunes. It was the way of things out here. What couldn't be fixed had to be endured, and you might as well paste a smile on your face while you were at it.

'No wonder you're so good with Bea.' He'd bet his last dollar that Charlie had had a hand in raising Wayne's sons.

She grinned as if she couldn't help it, and he found himself wanting to grin back. 'We call them the Dudleys—Dylan, Dominic and Davy. They were full of beans as little kids—into everything—and still have way too much energy, but they're lots of fun. Keeping an eye on them hasn't been a hardship.'

She loved them with every bit of herself, he could tell, and he found himself oddly envious. 'So who's managing Melaleuca now?'

'Pop with Mum's help. Uncle Wayne and his wife run their own web design business now. Though they still live at the station.'

Her grandfather had to be in his seventies. Why wasn't Charlie home on the station, helping out?

'We've had a run of bad luck at Melaleuca, which is why I'm at Kings Reach for the season.' She shrugged. 'My wage will help ease some of the pressure.'

No wonder Fitz had told him he'd need to guarantee Charlie's wage for the whole season. She couldn't afford not to work. Here he was, furious with Fraser for wanting to break the irrevocable trust, but he and his brothers weren't going to be left in straitened financial circumstances. They weren't in danger of losing the station. *Unless Jack sells it.* And *that* was definitely on the cards.

He shook the thought away. 'You know what I can't work out?'

'What's that?'

'How come we've never met?'

She blew on her hot chocolate. 'We probably have and just don't remember it. Six years doesn't make much difference now, but when I was fifteen, you'd have been twenty-one. I expect we were interested in different things, and hung out with very different people.'

That was true enough.

'Plus Mum and Fraser had a falling out when I was younger, which meant they avoided each other for years.'

'What did they fall out over?'

'My father. He worked here for a bit and Fraser fired him. My mother told Fraser *exactly* what she thought about that and what she thought of him. You can imagine how Fraser took that.' She sipped hot chocolate. 'In that instance, though, Fraser was right.'

There was something in the way she said *in that instance* that made him think it wasn't the only disagreement between the neighbours over the years.

'My father was an unreliable, selfish snake in the grass.'

'Not a fan of the man, then.'

'When I was six he decided country life was

too hard, took all our savings and left for the city. He left us behind and never looked back.'

A cold hand gripped his heart. Her father had *abandoned* her?

'After the divorce, my mother changed her surname and mine straight back to Ashwell. And then there was Connor Adams too—he's another reason we mightn't have met.'

The name was vaguely familiar.

'My childhood sweetheart. Connor and I met when we were fifteen. I was madly in love with him. So at the various social functions where we might've chanced to meet, I was too busy sneaking off with him.'

'Where's Connor now?'

'Who knows?'

Her shrug, though, was too casual. Things inside of him pulled tight. Jagged edges chafed at him.

'Probably somewhere in Brisbane.'

'How long were you guys together?'

She remained silent for so long he didn't think she was going to answer. 'Ten years.'

'*Ten years?*' That was longer than his marriage had lasted. 'Was he the one who broke his promises?'

She stared at him with eyes that had turned cold and distant. He rolled his shoulders. 'Earlier today you said it was one of the things that made you angry.'

'You know what, I'm getting sleepy.' She rose. 'Time for me to hit the sack.'

Rinsing out her mug, she left it on the drainer to dry. He watched her leave. Message received loud and clear. Connor Adams wasn't a topic up for discussion.

Tom found it hard to settle to anything the following day. After a series of early morning meetings, he sent a meme to the brothers' group chat of a little kid with his face smooshed up against a window captioned: Where are y'all?, before settling in to make a start on his projections. He'd show Fraser exactly how much a potential lawsuit would cost.

An hour later he stared at the figures in front of him and shook his head. It'd run into hundreds of thousands of dollars. What did Fraser hope to achieve? His father had never been reckless with money. Why would he pit the brothers against each other like this?

Not content with tearing the family apart once, he wanted to do it again? He thrust out his jaw. He, Logan and Fitz *would* stand with each other. They were *brothers*.

And Jack?

He dropped his head to the desk. Who knew? Jack hadn't responded to any of the messages on the group chat, hadn't returned any of Tom's calls.

After lunch he tried his darnedest to get back to work—to focus and concentrate, be productive—

but a pair of dancing blue eyes kept popping into his mind. What kind of fun were Bea and Charlie having this very moment. Hopscotch? A picnic down at the waterhole? Maybe they'd found a set of skittles or a frisbee.

He'd taken to working in the library—one of Fitz's favourite haunts—in the hopes of running into his brother. As a strategy it had proven singularly unsuccessful. He pushed out of his chair. This was pointless. He'd go and spend some time with his daughter.

And Charlie.

The words whispered through him with the teasing temptation of a siren's song. And every bit as dangerous. *Not* Charlie. He'd spend the afternoon with Bea. Charlie could spend some time tending to her horses and dogs.

That moment on the blanket yesterday…the way she'd stared at him when she'd made hot chocolates last night—as if she were starving and he was the only person who could satisfy her hunger—had him going hot and hard all over.

He couldn't give in to this. He'd fallen for Madeline after his mother died, when he'd been lost and alone. When his world had been in a spin. When he'd felt rootless and untethered. He wasn't repeating *that* mistake.

In hindsight he could see how a hefty dose of lust had clouded his judgement. Madeline had been one of the most beautiful women he'd ever clapped eyes on. But she'd made him laugh too, had made him feel the world could be a bright and happy place again. He'd seized on that with the strength of a drowning man.

It had taken two years for the scales to fall from his eyes. The funny thing was, nothing Madeline did had changed. She'd remained exactly the same. He'd just started to see her for who she was rather than who he'd wanted her to be. If he hadn't been wealthy, she'd never have shown the bad judgement to fall in love with him.

Their marriage hadn't become a battleground, but they hadn't wanted the same things, hadn't shared the same values, and he knew he disappointed her. The suffocating sense of feeling trapped, of not being able to breathe, the grief of lost dreams, all rose up through him now. At the time it had felt as if the very life was being squeezed from him

Madeline had told him she was pregnant before he could ask for a divorce. He'd abandoned all thoughts of a divorce after that unable to bear the thought of not being a full-time father, and he didn't regret it. Bea had been a joy. Madeline had only lived for another two years after Bea's birth. He was glad he hadn't created disharmony in the short time she'd had left.

But he'd learned his lesson. He'd have never been taken in by Madeline if he'd been more circumspect—if he hadn't *wanted* to believe in her so badly. He wouldn't make the same mistake now. His life had been thrown into turmoil since

Fraser's announcement. He wasn't going to grab onto the nearest source of solace and imagine it was something solid.

He didn't need solace. He just needed to keep his head. Reaching for his hat, he headed towards the cattle yards.

He found Bea and Charlie in one of the sorting yards. The same one where he and his brothers had learned to handle cattle. Where they'd practised their barrel racing and how to cut a yearling from a herd. Probably where he'd learned to ride too, though he couldn't remember that. He did remember him and Jack teaching Fitz and Will, though.

The child on a horse in this instance was Bea. He rested a hand on the top rail, his heart doing funny things in his chest. Charlie held a lead rein, giving soft instructions that his daughter followed to the letter. Bea beamed…utterly at home on the pony. He'd felt that same way once.

When had he—?

'She has a good seat.' Fitz came up beside him, nudging his shoulder.

'You get that pony in for her?'

'Seemed a good thing to do.' Fitz glanced across. 'That okay?'

He blew out a breath, nodded. 'Thanks, Fritzy.' He used the old childish nickname. 'It's perfect.'

'Anything for a kid of yours, Tombola.'

Which flashed him back twenty years and made him grin. *Now* would be the perfect time to bail his little brother up for a serious discussion, but Fraser's machinations and the threat looming over them momentarily receded in importance, making him reshuffle his priorities. He would *not* let it overshadow what was truly important—*family*.

It had been a long time since he'd felt any real connection with Fraser, but his brothers…? Well, that was another matter entirely. He *wanted* to solidify those bonds. He wanted *that* more than he wanted the station.

Fitz nudged him again. 'How long since you've been in the saddle? I remember a time when you spent more time on your horse than not.'

Tom shoved his hands in his pockets. Too long.

Bea's lesson came to an end and he watched as she learned how to brush her pony down. He and Fitz started along the fence towards her when Bea's voice drifted on the air. 'Charlie?'

'What's up, Honey Bea?'

'Do you know why Grandad doesn't like me?'

Charlie's head rocked back—not that he blamed her. *Dammit*. Why did this matter so much to Bea? And damn Fraser too. Why wasn't he making more of an effort with his granddaughter?

'I'm sure he does like you, sweetie.' Charlie kept grooming on her side of the pony. 'The thing is, with some of the older men out here they don't know how to talk to little girls…or little boys either, come to think of it.'

'Why not?'

'I guess they're out of practice. There aren't so many people out here to practice on.' Charlie rested her arms on the pony's back to peer across at Bea. 'Let me think on it a bit and see if we can't come up with a plan.'

'Okay.' Bea's voice lightened and he could've hugged Charlie for her lack of drama.

'Afternoon, ladies.' Fitz moved across to scratch the pony's head through the fence. 'Did Rambo mind his manners?'

Charlie nodded. 'The perfect gentleman.'

'I rode, Daddy! Did you see?'

Bea beamed at him and his chest did that funny bittersweet clenching thing it sometimes did around his daughter. 'I sure did. You're a natural.'

'Now, how's this for a plan, Buzzy Bea?' Fitz said, shooting Tom a sly glance. 'Why don't you and I find those puppies I told you about while Charlie and your dad take Cranky Frank and Lady Trippy out for a ride?'

What the hell? Wait. No way!

He...

Tom stretched his neck to the right and then the left. 'Cranky Frank?'

CHAPTER FIVE

Fitz wanted her to take Tom *riding*?

Charlie glanced between the two men. Was Fitz deliberately pushing them together? Fitz's lips twitched. 'What? Both your horses need exercising. Two birds, one stone.'

True, but she hadn't expected to exercise them *with Tom*.

Tom stared at Fitz in an equally befuddled manner. Fitz nudged him. 'And it seems to me Charlie's helped you out. Time to return the favour.'

Tom looked uncomfortable, which stung. He clearly didn't want to be alone with her.

Can you blame him after the way you walked out last night?

It wasn't her ridiculous overreaction last night to Tom's questions about Connor that sprang to mind now, but that moment on the blanket when she and Tom had nearly kissed. She had to stop thinking about that. She needed to get things between them back to normal.

He was a man under a lot of stress and she

didn't want to add to it. And one of her favourite stress releases was a good canter.

She made her lips prim and prissy. In a hopefully *humorous* way. 'Can he ride?'

Tom rolled his eyes. Fitz grinned. 'Put him on Cranky Frank. That will put him through his paces.'

She bit back a smile of her own and channelled all of the twinkly cheeriness she'd used on the Dudleys when they were little. 'Well, Tom, the pay is good if that's a consideration—all the milk and cookies you can eat, as well as a very pretty crayon drawing for your wall.'

Tom huffed out a laugh. 'And that's me sold to the highest bidder.' And damn it if her heart didn't go bumpity-bump.

Ten minutes later she and Tom were saddled up and heading in the direction of the river. All around them native grasses swayed in the soft breeze, creating the rippling rivers of gold that had helped to make Kings Reach one of the richest cattle stations in Australia. Red gums, shady and grand, followed the line of the river in the distance, looking closer than they actually were—distances could be deceptive out here. Far off to the left a ridge of red rock stretched up into the sky to where Fitz's ecotourist cabins were situated with their glorious views of the surrounding countryside.

Both of her horses were beautifully behaved, but she could feel Lady's eagerness in the bunched muscles beneath her thighs and her dancing side-steps. Frank would be the same. Tom looked as if he'd been born on a horse. His relaxed-but-ready grip, the loose shoulders and that straight back… not to mention those long legs.

Stop looking.

'Up for a canter?' she asked.

'Race you to the river?'

His smile had some of the shadows retreating from his eyes. It'd be nice to keep them at bay for as long as possible.

Why?

Why not? Some instinct told her Tom deserved a break—a proper break—maybe even needed one. And what the hell…? It'd be a nice thing to do. It didn't have to mean *anything.*

'Charlie?'

Oh! He was waiting for her answer. Her horses, her rules. 'It wouldn't be particularly fair.'

A teasing eyebrow kinked. ''Fraid I'll beat you?'

Which made her laugh. 'Not a chance. I know my horses. I'll give you a three-second start. At the eight-second mark, watch as I overtake you.'

He took off. It took all her strength to hold Lady back, but the moment she let her have her head the mare accelerated like a rocket. At seven seconds, rather than let her overtake and leave Tom and Frank in the dust, she eased Lady into a canter beside them.

Charlie gave herself up to the exhilaration of

the ride—the wind in her face, the motion of the horse beneath her, and all the colours and scents of the afternoon. They startled a flock of galahs when they reached the river, the birds lifting in a cloud of grey and pink, making Lady toss her head and dance. Frank didn't bat an eyelid. Slowing the horses, they veered to the right to amble beneath the sprawling branches of the gums, all four of them breathing hard.

Tom blew out a breath. 'I can't remember the last time I did that.'

The light in his eyes told her he'd enjoyed every moment. 'A good canter always puts the world to rights—at least it does for me. It's like meditation. When you're cantering, your mind empties of everything except the rhythm of the hoofbeats and the sounds around you and the scents of...'

She broke off, her cheeks heating, but Tom nodded.

'It's one of my favourite things in the world,' she mumbled.

'It used to be one of mine too.'

Then why had he left it so long between rides? She didn't ask—didn't want to stray into territory that might be too personal. She and Tom could be friendly, as long as they didn't become *too* friendly.

With that in mind, she fished out the toy soldier from her jeans pocket. She'd found it this morning in the dresser's secret compartment. She'd laughed at its oblique reference to her fluffy robe when she'd discovered it.

He grinned. 'Did you find the other one?'

'Not yet, but it's only a matter of time.'

'I like your confidence.'

'I'm a woman of action…'

'Not a cowpat,' he finished for her.

They both laughed, and despite her best intentions Charlie found herself relaxing.

'Why didn't you overtake me and beat me to the finishing line?'

The question made her blink. 'I…'

'Did you think I'd be a sore loser?'

Her face heated.

'You did!'

'Not really. I just… Habit, I suppose. The Dudleys all went through phases of having their noses put out of joint if I beat them. Some days it just wasn't worth the hassle.' Connor hadn't liked it either. She pushed a stray strand of hair behind her ear. 'Besides, it didn't feel like a real race—just a bit of fun.'

Reaching across, he pulled Lady to a halt. She stared at his forearm and fought the urge to trace its muscled contours. Her thighs clenched, Lady danced and fidgeted, and she forced them to relax again, forced herself to meet Tom's gaze.

'Don't diminish yourself for anyone, Charlie. You don't need to do that. Especially not with me. It's not your job to make up for others' shortfalls.'

'Okay.' The word squeaked out of her and he

released Lady's reins, and as both horses moved forward she found she could breathe again—after a fashion—though her pulse refused to return to normal.

'So Cranky Frank isn't fast…*or* particularly cranky.'

She bit back a grin. 'To his credit, though, he can canter all day if you need him to. And his action is so smooth. It's like being on a giant rocking horse. He's a perfect gentleman.'

'While Lady Trippy Fast Feet…?'

'Is fleet of foot, has a bouncier action, and will hopefully one day have manners to match Frank's.'

His laugh almost made her feel as good as the canter had. He ran a hand down Frank's neck and she shivered. Beneath her shirt, her nipples hardened. 'They're beautiful horses, Charlie.'

She pulled her gaze away. 'We've been breeding our own horses at Melaleuca for a long time. I chose both Frank's and Lady's sire and dam.' Her grandfather had trusted her, and she'd been determined not to let him down. 'I was still a teenager when Frank was born. He's going on eleven. While Lady is a youngster of five.'

'A Jill of all trades,' he mused. 'I really am underutilising your talents, aren't I?'

'No!' The word shot out of her too quickly and with too much force. She tried to moderate her tone, hoped to God her smile eased his concerns and any suspicions she might've just unwittingly raised. 'A change is as good as a holiday. I'm enjoying hanging out with Bea. She's great fun.' Both of those things were true.

'She enjoys hanging out with you too. You're great with her.' He paused. 'I'm surprised, given all of your station experience, that Fitz urged me to poach you from Perry.'

'I'm not. He adores Bea and he trusts me. Nothing will be more important to him than making sure Bea is safe.'

Tom pursed his lips, nodded. 'You're right.' He was silent for a moment. 'If you've known Fitz since you were kids then you must've known Will too.'

Her heart clenched at the pain that briefly flashed through his eyes. 'Not as well as Fitz—the two of us were horse mad.' Will could ride as well as the rest of them, but he'd preferred other things more—birdwatching, identifying the dizzying array of insects that populated the Kimberley, painting. 'I remember him being a really good guy, though. He taught me how to draw a horse one rainy afternoon at camp, when I was feeling bored. I've never forgotten it.'

She didn't add anything stupid like *You must miss him*, or anything of that ilk. Of course Tom missed his brother.

Tom intercepted the look she surreptitiously sent him and raised an eyebrow. She grimaced. 'While we're on the subject of family, Bea mentioned something about her grandfather.'

'I heard.'

She tried not to grimace. 'Would it be okay with you if I helped to…bridge the distance a little? I promise not to leave Bea alone and unsupervised.' She hadn't forgotten *that* instruction.

'I…'

Tom dragged a hand through his hair, the expression in his eyes making her heart tumble. 'Look, I know family can be complicated. Whatever your answer, I know you'll have your reasons. Reasons you *don't* have to share with me. No judgement here. It's just… Your relationship with Fraser and Bea's relationship with him will likely be very different.'

She might not like Fraser, but it didn't change the fact that he was Bea's grandfather. She couldn't imagine life without her Pop. If Bea could have even a fraction of that relationship with her grandfather… Well, it was worth fighting for.

Tom remained silent. Smothering a sigh, she shrugged. 'It was just a thought. Forget it. I'm probably biased, as my grandfather is my hero.'

'Your grandfather is one of the good guys.'

Meaning Fraser wasn't?

'I don't want Bea getting her hopes up and being hurt.'

'I don't want that either.' She thought for a moment. 'When Fraser returns, do you think I could continue eating with the family?' For the last two nights, Bea had insisted Charlie join her, Tom and Fitz for dinner. 'That way you can see my attempts in action and will have an opportunity to close them down if you want to.'

She watched him chew over her words. She didn't understand the source of the tension between Tom and his father. She didn't know if it was recent or long-standing. 'What was Fraser like when you were Bea's age?'

For a moment something in his eyes lightened. 'He was always a man of few words, but he showed me how things worked. Whenever I wanted to learn something, he'd teach me.' He rubbed a hand over a jaw that had darkened intriguingly. 'Jack and I were mad about cricket and he'd spend hours showing us how to hold a ball, how to bowl leg spinners, how to steal a quick run.'

Tom blinked as long-ago memories flooded him. 'He took us to a one-day game in Perth once—Jack, me and Logan. I'd have been ten. Australia played Pakistan. We won by seven wickets. It was the most exciting day of my life.'

'Is that when you fell in love with the city?'

He shook his head. He'd never fallen in love with the city, though it seemed daft to say as much. 'I loved growing up out here.' At least he had, until everything had gone to hell in a handbasket after Will's death.

'What's it like being back?'

Charlie dismounted and he did his absolute best

not to notice the sweet curves of her backside. He could imagine cupping those curves all too clearly and—

Frank stamped a foot and Tom blinked himself back into the moment. Reaching for his common sense, he dismounted too. Looping Frank's reins around a nearby sapling as Charlie had done with Lady's, he followed her down to the riverbank.

The late-afternoon sun slanted down through the leaves of the trees, turning the wide, slow-moving river orange. Charlie gestured at the view—vast, ancient, timeless. 'It's beautiful.'

A mob of kangaroos bounded into view on the other side of the river, spreading out to crop the grass. Not a single man-made sound intruded on the birdsong or the sound of the river. Not a single man-made structure could be seen from this vantage point. She was right. It *was* beautiful.

'I don't know how you can bear to stay away.'

Charlie too was edged with the golden glow of the afternoon light, her blonde curls fiery like the embers in a campfire, her tanned skin giving off a warm glow that heated his blood. 'Never been tempted to leave?'

She shook her head and picked her way down to the river's edge. Across the water the red buck in charge of the mob rose up on its hind legs to stare at them. 'My grandmother had a copy of Heidi that I read when I was a girl.'

She settled on a large rock, patting the spot beside her. He silently sat. When he glanced across the river again, the buck had resumed eating.

'Heidi lived on a mountain in Switzerland. When she was forced to leave and live in the valley, she became homesick and her health started to fail. When she was able to return to her mountain, she became well again.' She glanced across and the smile she sent him pierced some invisible barrier around his heart. 'That's how I feel about this place.'

He knew she wasn't referring specifically to Kings Reach, but to the Kimberley itself.

'I don't feel as if I could be as happy anywhere else. I don't feel as if I'd ever fit in anywhere else.'

'I think you'd fit in wherever you went, Charlie. You're great company—fun, funny, warm… kind. Adaptable. And you're competent at everything you turn your hand to. People would like you wherever you went.'

Blue eyes blinked up into his. 'I…'

He fought a smile at her bamboozled expression. 'But I know what you mean.' He'd felt that way himself once. He turned to take in the view. 'I'm shocked at how much I'm enjoying being back.'

But now with Fraser threatening to take this place away from him… His hands clenched. He wanted a say in the future of Kings Reach. He wanted the freedom to return here whenever the mood took him, and to stay for as long as he damn well pleased. He wanted…

To return for good?

He turned the words over in his mind before shaking them off. He had a life in Sydney—a gorgeous Victorian terrace in a swanky inner-city suburb, a thriving financial firm, friends. Bea had her school, her friends, her Uncle Logan.

Charlie nudged him and pointed to a barramundi that foraged in the water in front of them. He blinked. 'If I had a fishing line…'

'Next time. There are plenty of them in the river.' Her eyes glowed. 'I love this time of year when the place is so full of life.' She gestured at the water, across the river to the grazing kangaroos and then skyward to where a huge wedgetail eagle circled on the air currents above. 'For the moment there's enough for everybody. And we can just…'

He found himself hanging on her words. *They could just…?* 'What?'

'Be happy.'

She smiled, and for the life of him he couldn't help smiling back. Even though he couldn't remember the last time he'd been so wholly and uncomplicatedly happy as Charlie was now.

Oh, there'd been high points—Bea's birth, for one. But at the same time he'd been trying to reconcile himself to a less than ideal marriage. He'd been reconciling himself to the less-than-ideal since before Will's death. For a moment, though, Charlie's smile chased those memories away and made him believe uncomplicated happiness could be within his reach—if he dared stretch out his hand.

'Yes.' He nodded in sudden decision. 'Okay, yes. If you think you can broker a relationship between Bea and Fraser I'm happy for you to try.'

She spun around with wide eyes, and then reached out to clasp his hand. 'You're a good man, Tom.'

Her smile had something magical circling around them. Her gaze lowered to his lips, the blue of her eyes darkening, and a now familiar heat built inside him. He could—

A duck honked and they both sprang to their feet. Charlie swiped her hands down the seat of her jeans, looking everywhere but at him. He swiped his forearm across his brow before re-settling his hat on his head.

Charlie pointed at the sun sinking in the west. 'Probably time to head back.'

He nodded. A helicopter sounded on the still air. Shading his eyes, Tom tracked its progress. Looked as if Fraser was home.

Charlie didn't waste any time. She made her first move during dinner that evening—which happened to be perfectly cooked sirloin steak, an enormous potato bake, and steamed vegetables. Steak and potatoes never tasted this good in the city. When she'd first joined the table, Fraser had raised an eyebrow in Tom's direction, and Tom had sent a pointed glance in Annalise's. His father's PA ate with the family, and thank God she did or there'd be next to no conversation.

'Did you tell your grandad what you did today, Honey Bea?' Charlie said.

Bea stared at Charlie before her eyes swung to her grandfather. 'I rode Rambo.'

Fraser halted mid-chew. With a considerable effort, he swallowed. 'Rambo, huh? Who's, uh, Rambo?'

'My pony!'

'You have a pony?'

'Uncle Fitz got him for me and he's the best.'

Fraser cleared his throat. 'Hold on, let me get this right, who's the best? Uncle Fitz or Rambo?'

Bea giggled. 'Rambo, silly.'

Good God. How would his father take to being called silly by a five-year-old? Fraser's lips twitched. 'Right. Got it straight in my head now.'

'Rambo is the best, and Uncle Fitz is *a cool dude*.'

Fitz choked, Charlie coughed to cover a laugh, and Tom grinned. Bea beamed, clearly loving having captured her grandfather's attention. An invisible fist squeezed his heart.

'Daddy said I'm a natural and Uncle Fitz said I'm going to be creating a ruckus soon. And Charlie said I wasn't a ruckus, but a force to be reckoned with.'

'I reckon they're all right.'

'And I'm going to ride your horse one day, Grandad, because Emperor *loves* me.'

Oho! This would be interesting. None of the boys had been allowed to ride Fraser's horse. Didn't mean they hadn't. But they'd sure as heck made sure he'd never found out.

Fraser just nodded. 'Emperor shows good judgement, then.'

Tom glanced across at Charlie and she sent him a cheeky wink. The woman was a miracle worker! An unexpected bubble of optimism lodged in his chest. Maybe, in drawing closer to his granddaughter, Fraser would see the damage he'd be doing in attempting to break the trust. After all, Kings Reach was her legacy too.

Tom came to a halt several afternoons later at the ruckus that greeted him in the foyer.

'I want to put it in there myself!' Bea had thrust her bottom lip out—never a good sign—and all but stamped her foot.

'I'm sorry, but—'

'Come on, Annalise.' Charlie raised both hands as if to silently say, *You can't be serious?* 'Bea has been working on this for two days.'

This was a cardboard horse on a stand. The horse looked suspiciously like Rambo, while the rider looked like Bea. He'd bet Charlie had drawn it and cut it out, though Bea was clearly the decorator. Sparkles and tinsel and colour abounded. She'd put a lot of effort into it. If she'd made it for him, he'd have treasured it forever.

'She wants to surprise her grandad with it.

Where's the harm in that?' Charlie said to Annalise.

'Orders are orders, Charlie. You know that.'

Charlie wrinkled her nose in acknowledgement—and probably sympathy—but she was a woman of action, not a cowpat. 'Seriously? She's five years old. What do you think she's going to do in there? Steal the family silver?'

He wouldn't mind knowing the answer to that himself.

Annalise, though, held firm. 'I'm sorry, ladies.'

What was it Charlie had called him when they'd first met—a prince of the realm? Maybe it was time to act like one? 'What's going on?'

Bea ran up to him. 'Annalise won't let me put this on Grandad's desk as a surprise!'

'You made this, Buzzy Bea?' He knelt down beside her.

She dragged in a big breath. 'It's a self-portrait on a pony,' she recited as if she'd memorised it.

Which she obviously had. He let out a low whistle. 'It's really something. Will you make me one too?'

Bea glanced at Charlie, who nodded. 'Yes,' her bottom lip wobbled, 'but this one is Grandad's.'

His father had done nothing to earn this. He pushed the unworthy thought aside and straightened, raising an eyebrow at Annalise in the way that made his underlings at the office quail. From the corner of his eye he saw Charlie smother a smile, which made him see the humour in the situation but probably diluted the eyebrow's effect because, unfortunately, he had no more luck shifting Annalise than either Bea or Charlie.

'Your father has given me specific instructions to not let anyone into his office.'

'Why not?'

'I'm not privy to his reasons, Tom—no more than Charlie is privy to yours. I merely follow his instructions.'

He had to admire her integrity. 'What if I need the financial records? It's tax time and I'm finalising the reports to send to the accountant.'

'If that's the case, I can ring your father to check.'

'Then can you ring him about this without totally giving away Bea's surprise?'

She did. The result was that Annalise was allowed to escort Bea into the office while he and Charlie waited outside. Charlie stood in the doorway beside him, her vanilla and eucalyptus scent rising up all around him, her eyes wide as if trying to take everything in. While he searched for whatever it was his father didn't want him to see.

With the job done, Bea raced out and threw herself into his arms. 'Thank you, Daddy.'

Charlie smiled up at him. 'My hero.' She feigned a swoon before winking and clapping her hands. 'Right, Bea, we have time for either hopscotch or quoits. Choose your poison.'

Charlie and Bea ambled off and he considered following, but his gaze caught on the curve of

Charlie's backside in those well-worn jeans—had any woman ever look better in a pair of jeans?—and reminded himself of all the reasons he needed to keep his distance.

Annalise locked the door once more and strode away. He stared at the heavy wood and tapped a finger against it. What was Fraser hiding?

On impulse, he checked the secret compartment in the dresser and pulled out a small plastic horse along with a note folded into the shape of a star. It read: *Tom, I understand you no longer have a horse here at Kings Reach—and at this time of year most of the horses will be busy or having a well-earned rest day. If you ever need a good canter to clear your head, you'd be doing me a great favour if you'd take out either Frank or Lady. They could do with the exercise.*

His heart leaped. She'd trust him with her horses? He folded the missive back into the shape of a star and put it in the left-hand pocket of his shirt and patted it twice, before setting off in the direction of the stables.

CHAPTER SIX

CHARLIE'S HEART THUNDERED in her ears as she knelt in front of Fraser's office door and used every bit of her recently acquired expertise on how to pick a lock. The internet was a wonderful thing. *Breathe, Charlie, breathe. Stop shaking. Don't get caught.*

This might be her one chance to make things right for Pop, but if she was caught… The thought of disappointing Tom, of watching his easy smile turn to derision, had her heart contracting like a screwed-up piece of tissue paper. *Tom doesn't matter.*

Except that he did. He was a good guy who was trusting her with his daughter and she'd hate him to think it had all been a lie. For a moment she was tempted to rise to her feet and go back to bed.

Squaring her shoulders, she gave herself a mental slap. *Think of Pop.*

The sound of the latch giving way echoed around the foyer. She didn't move until she was certain no one was coming to investigate.

Slipping inside the room, she closed the door

and locked it behind her. Using the torch on her phone, she moved towards two enormous filing cabinets. Bless Tom for getting Bea's *self-portrait on a pony* into the room. At least it had given her a peek at the layout and an idea of where to centre her search.

Pulling open the top drawer of the first filing cabinet, she flicked through the meticulously tabbed files. She'd started to close it when a key scratched in the lock of the door. Her heart lurched into her throat. Her pulse raced like a wild thing. Shoving her phone into her pocket, she dived behind an armchair and made herself as small as possible, tried to breathe as quietly as possible.

If she was caught…

She rested her head on her knees and squished her eyes shut. Eventually she opened one. The lights hadn't been turned on. A light similar to the one on her phone flitted about the room. Had someone else broken into Fraser's office?

As carefully as she could, she peered around the chair…to discover the long, lean lines of a figure moving towards Fraser's desk. She eased back. *Tom.* Tom had broken into his father's office. *Why?*

The why doesn't matter. If he finds you you're done for.

She crossed her fingers. *Please, don't let him find me.*

The squeak of him sitting in Fraser's chair

made her start. There was no chance she'd make it to the door unseen. She'd have to sit tight and hope for the best.

The office door crashed back on its hinges, making her jump. She flinched when the overhead light came on.

'You want to explain what you're doing?'

Fraser! Oh, God, she was doomed.

'Wondering what the hell is so top-secret I needed to gain *permission* for your granddaughter to put something she'd made for you *especially*—something she was proud and excited about—on your desk to surprise you.'

Fraser remained silent for two beats. 'I knew that'd get your goat.'

It was an expression Pop used as well. *Get your goat.* It had her spine stiffening. The two men had *nothing* in common. Pop was honourable, and it irked some sense of justice inside her that they should share even as much as a common vocabulary. Even if she did get caught, she wasn't going down without a fight. Her hands clenched. She'd fight tooth and nail for Pop and Melaleuca Downs.

Still, it'd be better *not* to be caught. *So stay where you are and don't make a sound.*

'I also figured that if I camped out in your office overnight I might finally get a chance to have that conversation with you. You know—the one you've been avoiding?'

His shadow on the wall sprawled back as if completely at its ease. She envied it desperately.

'The one you've been doing your damnedest to avoid since the night of the ball.' The chair squeaked again as Tom straightened.

'I thought I'd made it perfectly clear that there's nothing to discuss.'

How convenient! Charlie scowled at Fraser's shadow. He always considered *his* the final word. He seemed to think he could get away with walking over everyone. *That* had to stop.

Tom shot to his feet and the chair slid back on its wheels to crash against the wall behind. 'You're proposing to tear this family apart and you don't think *that's* worth discussing?'

Fraser was doing *what*? She risked a peek around the chair at Tom. His blazing eyes and flared nostrils made her swallow.

'What do you care anyway?' Fraser shouted. The suddenness of it made her flinch and duck further behind her chair. 'You've barely been back to Kings Reach since your mother died!'

'And yet—' she didn't understand the mockery in Tom's voice '—it's more times than Jack's been home.'

Fraser said nothing and Tom gave a harsh laugh. 'And now we get to the hypocritical heart of the matter, don't we? The hypocritical heart of *you*, Fraser.'

She had no idea what they were talking about. Whatever it was, though, it was hurting Tom badly and she had to clench her hands to stop herself from rising up against Fraser in some kind of Mama Bear fashion that she was damn sure Tom wouldn't appreciate.

'Look, Tom, you four boys will all get an equal share in the station. You're not losing out financially, so I don't see what the problem is. Sign the damn paperwork and let's move on.'

'Not a chance, old man. If we sign that paperwork we no longer get an equal say in what happens at Kings Reach. You can shove your money where the sun don't shine. What *I* care about is Fitz. Have you even given him a second thought? He's the only one of us to make a life here. He's built a thriving ecotourism business and you're prepared to put all of that at risk?'

'I know what I'm doing!'

She went to rub at her face, but lowered her hand. *Don't make a sound.* She wished herself miles away. She wished herself home at Melaleuca, where her family loved and supported each other.

Tom's shadow on the wall lifted a file before letting it drop back to the desk. 'We won't be signing your paperwork, Fraser. We'll be fighting you with everything we have. I've put together an estimate of what a lawsuit will cost the station. *If* you're interested. Bring an end to this madness while you still can.'

Her eyes bugged. A lawsuit? Good God.

Fraser took the file, along with another one sitting on top of his desk. 'I'm doing what's best for Kings Reach, son. I wish you would trust me.'

'I haven't trusted you since I was fourteen years old.'

She pressed a hand to her mouth to stifle a gasp. If Tom ever spoke to her in that tone she'd want to die. Fraser spun on his heel and left the room as if he didn't trust himself to remain a moment longer. When his steps had receded, Tom swore and collapsed back in the chair.

Her heart burned—her stomach burned; so did her throat. *Stay where you are. Don't make a sound.*

She peeked around the chair. Tom sat with his head in his hands and the defeated slope of his shoulders speared into the sorest part of her. The lump in her throat grew so big the ache of it stretched into her temples. *Oh, Tom.* Before she could think better of it, she slid out from behind the chair and stood up.

Tom sent her a sidelong glance and then gave a slow blink, straightening. She gave a tiny wave. 'Surprise.'

'What—?'

'I'll explain all that in a minute.' She moved across to the desk, her fingers fidgeting with its edge. 'Are you okay?'

Those grey eyes throbbed into hers and for a moment he looked so lost and alone she had to fight the urge to pull him into a hug. If she hugged him, it could so easily turn into something more. *Much* more. There were already too many high emotions zinging around. It wouldn't be wise to add more to the mix.

His shoulders sagged. 'I'm not sure I've ever missed my mother more than I do right now.'

'You guys were close?'

He nodded.

'I am with mine too. Don't know what I'd do without her.' She moved around the desk and took his arm, hauled him to his feet. 'Come on, let's get out of here.'

'You haven't told me what you're actually doing here yet.'

'I will. I'll tell you a bedtime story that will curl your toes.' She pulled him towards the door. 'But let's do that over a hot chocolate.'

'I've got a better idea.' He grabbed the decanter of brandy from the sideboard.

'Perfect.' She dropped his arm to grab two crystal tumblers and followed him as he led the way upstairs to their little sitting room. He sat at one end of the sofa and poured the brandy. She grabbed two spare blankets—nights at this time of year could be surprisingly chilly—and dropped one in his lap before snuggling up beneath hers at the other end of the sofa.

He handed her a brandy, but all of his earlier lost-ness had disappeared, replaced with a cool-eyed watchfulness that had her stomach churning. Had she been an idiot to reveal her presence downstairs? Damn it. She should've thought things through more thoroughly. It was just… If any of the Dudleys ever looked as bereft and defeated as Tom had just done, she'd want someone to offer them comfort and friendship; to make sure they didn't feel so alone.

She'd been an idiot to forget one thing, though. Tom was a King of Kings Reach. He and his father might be having a difference of opinion at the moment, and they might not even be close in the way her family was close, but they were still family. If forced to choose a side, his father or the right thing to do, which would Tom choose?

Exhaustion settled over her like a dusty saddle blanket. *Guess we're about to find out.*

He raised his tumbler in a silent toast and they both sipped their brandy. She was no connoisseur, but the smooth heat that slipped down her throat to warm her belly had her eyes widening. Tom's lips kicked up as if he could read her surprise and found it…

Actually, she didn't know what that wry twist of his lips meant, but one thing she did know was that she didn't want to try his patience. Regardless of who he chose and what he chose to do about it, *she* was honourable, and she'd promised him the truth.

Setting her tumbler on the coffee table, she hugged the blanket around her more fully and pulled in a breath. 'Once upon a time on an outback cattle station in the heart of the Kimberley called Melaleuca Downs…'

His eyes never left her face. 'Your home.'

Something in her chest fractured. 'My home.'

Things inside Tom hardened as Charlie narrated her story. Despite the fairy-tale framework, she told it without embellishment or exaggeration, which only served to highlight Fraser's ruthlessness. And he didn't doubt a word of it. Not a single one.

'Fraser promised to lease that land to your grandfather for a fair price, and then waited until the new stock had arrived at Melaleuca before reneging on the deal?'

'Yep.'

She reached for her brandy, her hand shaking, and Tom had to grit his teeth and count to three before he could trust his voice. The thought of anyone taking advantage of Charlie and her family had him wanting to tear things apart with his bare hands.

This shouldn't matter so much to you.

It shouldn't matter so much to him *personally*, but that was a separate issue. As a man who prided himself on ethical business practices, what his father had done was abhorrent. 'Why hasn't your grandfather made a hullabaloo? Gone public? Hired lawyers?' Sid Ashwell was well-respected.

'Melaleuca is small fry compared to Kings Reach. We've created a specialist herd that's in high demand and fetches an excellent price on the market, and our reputation is growing. But we suffered a lot of damage in last year's bushfires, there were Nanna's recent hospital bills, and then we were landed with an unexpected tax bill due to an accounting error.'

He made a note to find out who their accountant was. That should never have happened. He'd recommend someone more reliable.

'But as we all know, that's how life on the land sometimes rolls. Although we didn't have much left in the coffers, we all agreed now was the right time to expand.' She glared into her brandy. 'Except…'

Except Fraser had reneged on the deal.

'We now have stock we can't afford to feed—'

'But you *are* feeding them?'

'Of course we are!' She looked shocked. 'But, Tom, we can ill afford it. And we don't have the resources to take on a giant like Kings Reach in a lawsuit. Nobody says it out loud, but your father would squash us like a bug.'

Acid burnt his throat. Two weeks ago he'd have had trouble believing Charlie's story. Two weeks ago he'd never have believed Fraser would make a move to break the irrevocable trust. He and his father might not be close, Fraser might have a temper and a reputation for being a hard-nosed businessman, but to the best of his knowledge Fraser's dealings had all been legitimate.

What did Tom really know about any of that, though? *His* job was to invest the profits, to create an investment portfolio that ensured the station's ongoing success. He'd done that, and he'd done it well, but he had no hand in his father's actual business dealings. 'Do you think he's after your station?' Was Fraser trying to bankrupt Melaleuca in an effort to get his hands on it at a cheap price?

'The thought had crossed my mind, but I can't think of a single reason why he would. We have some of the best grazing land in the country, but so does Kings Reach. Kings Reach has grazing land it's not using.'

He rubbed a hand over his face. 'What were you going to do with the contract once you'd found it?'

Beneath the blanket, one shoulder lifted. She looked lost and alone. He had to fight an urge to pull her into his arms and tell her everything would be okay. He had no right making such promises. His hands clenched. But nor would he allow her family to suffer at his father's hands.

But once the thought of holding Charlie had entered his mind, he couldn't rid himself of the images his imagination supplied. A deep thirst gripped him. To feel her soft curves pressed against his body, to breathe in the scent of her, to feel her hands slide across his bare flesh. Heat bubbled in his veins.

'I planned to confront your father with it— shame him into fulfilling his side of the bargain,' she said, completely oblivious to the war that raged inside of him.

He did his best to keep his face opaque. Breathed through the ache of desire and temptation.

Her lips twisted. 'You think that naïve. But I'd at least give the man a chance to do the right thing. If he refused, then I'd make the document public. Out here a man's reputation is everything. I might not be able to afford fancy lawyers, but I have access to social media, and I'm well known out here—respected. As is my grandfather.'

Out here a man's reputation did matter. There would be people—important people—who'd refuse to do business with Fraser if that kind of word got out, whether it could be proven or not. No smoke without fire and all that. And when that word came from such a respected source as the Ashwells...

A plan took shape in his mind. Not a *nice* plan. But as his father no longer played nicely, as evidenced by his dealings with Melaleuca, or wouldn't see reason, as evidenced by his determination to break the irrevocable trust, Tom wasn't sure he ought to have qualms about the *niceness* of his plan. *Fight fire with fire.*

Pressing fingers to his eyes, he finally had to acknowledge what he could no longer ignore. 'You lied to me.' An ache lodged beneath his breastbone. Charlie had taken the job he'd offered her under false pretences. She'd *lied* to him.

He understood why she'd done it. She had no reason to trust him—he was a King of Kings Reach, for God's sake—but it left a bitter taste in his mouth all the same. He'd thought her the opposite of Madeline, but perhaps they weren't so different after all. It was a dog-eat-dog world, and in both cases he felt as if he'd been the bone. He'd been forced to make the best of his situation with Madeline, but he didn't have to do so with Charlie now.

'Yes. I lied to you.'

He waited for her to justify herself. And kept right on waiting. 'Is that all you're going to say?'

She set her brandy down, met his gaze. 'You know why I've done what I've done. Trying to sugar-coat it feels wrong. And I wouldn't expect you to believe me anyway.'

'Try me.' He wasn't sure who was more surprised by his words—himself or Charlie.

Her chin squared in that unconscious way she had when she was being a *woman of action*. 'I'm not going to lie to you, Tom. When you offered me the position of Bea's nanny, one of the first things I thought about was how it would give me better access to Fraser's office. To pretend otherwise would be an insult to your intelligence, but...'

He held his breath.

'What I doubt you'll believe is that I'd have taken the job anyway.'

She was right. He didn't believe her.

'Kids, horses and dogs—I'm a sucker for the lot of them. Bea is great.' She glanced in the direction of Bea's bedroom, a soft smile curving her lips, and his heart caught. 'I've loved every moment I've spent with her—she's a great kid and you've every right to be proud of her.' Her gaze moved back to him. 'But that's the part you won't believe. You'll think I'm trying to soften you up so I can stay.'

Bingo. Except…she *had* been great with Bea. Their friendship wasn't feigned. She and Bea had clicked the way some people did.

'I'm truly sorry I betrayed your trust, Tom.'

He fought a frown. 'There are a couple of things I don't understand.'

'Such as?'

'You can't have a good opinion of Fraser.'

'I think he's loathsome.'

'So why would you promote any kind of relationship between him and Bea?'

She reached for her glass, stared into it. 'While Fraser might be loathsome to everyone else, I expect he's very different with his family.'

Which went to show what she knew about it.

'And, as I told you—my grandfather is my hero. If Bea can have even a fraction of a relationship like that with Fraser it'd be worthwhile. Anyway,' her chin squared again, 'the more people you can love in your life, the better.'

'As long as they love you back.'

She bit her lip and nodded.

'Why didn't you remain hidden in Fraser's office, Charlie?' She hadn't needed to reveal herself. 'I'd have left and been none the wiser. So *why*?'

'Because I'm an idiot,' she muttered.

Why the hell would she have given herself away like that?

She scowled. 'Look, Tom, I've no idea what's going on between you and your father—and I don't need to know.' Her scowl deepened. 'And I'm no gossip, so you needn't think I'll be mentioning what I overheard to anyone.'

'I didn't think you would.' Which seemed odd when a moment ago he'd felt so bitter about the fact she'd lied to him. She could make a pretty packet if she went to the papers with the story—enough to feed her cattle for a month—but even as he thought it, he knew she wouldn't do it.

Shaking herself out from beneath the blanket, she strode across to the balcony doors and stared up at the sky—as if finding familiar constellations and stars to ground herself. Eventually she turned. 'I didn't understand half of what you and Fraser flung at each other tonight, but after he left you looked…'

He moved to stand in front of her. 'I looked…?'

She stared at a point in the middle of his chest. 'Alone,' she murmured. 'Very alone. I know what that feels like.'

His hands clenched. *Who* had made her feel like that?

'And I…'

She…?

One shoulder lifted. 'I wanted you to know you had at least one friend—that you didn't have to feel so alone.'

She'd betrayed her presence because she'd been *concerned for him*?

Her chin lifted. 'And that's the truth, although you won't believe it.'

He bent at the waist to stare more fully into her face. She squared her shoulders and swallowed, but her gaze didn't drop from his. For the briefest of moments her eyes flicked to his mouth. She swallowed. The pulse in her throat thrashed out a staccato rhythm.

Fire swept along his nerve endings. 'The thing is, Charlie, I do believe you.' And he did.

Her head rocked back, but the two of them remained connected by an invisible thread that bound them tight. The scent of vanilla and eucalyptus engulfed him, as if her shock had sent it rolling off her in waves. 'You do?'

Charlie wasn't some villain out for all she could get. She was a good person who was trying to protect her family. 'Yes.'

'Why?'

'Bea likes you. Your bond with her isn't a figment of my imagination.'

Her hands went to her hips. 'Bea is a five-year-old, Tom. She's not yet a sterling judge of character.'

He swallowed back a laugh. 'Are you telling me not to believe you?'

'I'm telling you not to use Bea's judgement as a basis for good decision-making.'

'Your horses and dogs love you. My brother thinks you're True Blue.' And out here True Blue was the highest of accolades. 'And my own instincts tell me you're not lying now. And, while it's also true that I may not be a sterling judge of character...'

Her smile hit him like an earthquake—full of relief and gladness. He swore the ground beneath his feet rocked. She looked as if she wanted to dance!

She moved a tiny step closer. 'But you're a grown-up,' she whispered.

'*Very* grown-up,' he assured her.

Very slowly her gaze tracked down his body and back up again, leaving him shaking and wanting. 'Very grown-up,' she agreed, an answering heat in her eyes. She moved a step closer. 'You really believe me, Tom?'

He couldn't drag his gaze from hers. Didn't want to. 'I really believe you.'

Her lips parted and her chest rose and fell. 'I could hug you.'

'Feel free.' His words emerged on a husky murmur, probably surprising them both.

The simmering tension charged into something fiercer. Charlie's scent wound about him like a promise. He wanted a taste so badly...

'This is madness,' she murmured, and yet he saw the exact moment she decided to throw caution to the wind.

He didn't move away. 'Total madness.'

'Permission to engage the enemy,' she whispered.

He couldn't resist. 'Permission granted.'

CHAPTER SEVEN

Tom believed her!

Charlie's chest billowed with something that made her feel light and free. She wanted to hug the world, to dance, sing…*and kiss Tom*. Sliding a hand behind his nape, she pulled his head down to meet hers…touched her lips to his.

And melted.

Tom kissed her back with warmth and heat and hunger and she could've wept at the sheer relief of it. She'd lied to him, and yet he still liked her. He *understood*. And it was such a gift!

Wrapping her arms around his neck, she pressed her body full-length against his and kissed him back in a way that should leave him in no doubt how extraordinary she thought him— not just hot and gorgeous, but fun and funny, kind and smart. And perfect.

He groaned into her mouth and gathered her close, those big hands roving over her shoulders and back and then down to cup her buttocks. She moved against him, restless, seeking an outlet for the hunger he'd ignited. Those fingers moved dangerously close to the spot that most hungered for his touch, making her gasp. He took full advantage of that to deepen the kiss. Sensation swamped her—thick, hot and dangerous, and so damn good she could cry.

Big hands beneath her buttocks lifted to press her against the hardness at the juncture of his thighs and she wrapped her legs around his waist and cursed the clothes in their way. The hot, wet kisses he pressed to her throat drove her half out of her mind. They were driving her to the edge of a precipice she had no intention of stepping back from.

With a growl, she tried to drag his T-shirt over his head. If she didn't touch bare skin soon she'd go mad. 'Hold on,' he ground out. He balanced her with one arm, and then the other as she pulled his T-shirt over first one arm and then the other and finally over his head.

'I think I stretched it.' She dropped it to the floor, her hands moving across strongly muscled shoulders and down over his chest, and everything inside her fluttered and clenched.

'Hell, Charlie.' His jaw clenched and he shuddered. 'I—'

She kissed him. She didn't want reality intruding. Not now. Lifting her head a moment later, she met his gaze and wondered if her eyes blazed as fiercely as his. 'I don't want to stop.'

'This is madness.' His breath was ragged, but he pressed her more firmly against his hardness and she flung her head back, her fingers digging into his shoulders as she swallowed a cry.

'I'll tell you what's madness,' she managed when she caught her breath, 'the fact I've never wanted anyone as much as I want you right now.'

With a growl, he captured her lips in another heated kiss that left her panting. 'My room.' She didn't know if it was an order or a plea, but could've wept when he immediately moved to her door. 'Condoms in the top drawer,' she got out before his mouth was once more on hers and she was blind and mindless to all else.

They tore off their clothes. She touched him everywhere—the strong masculine lines of him filling her with awe. His hands touched her everywhere, making her want in a way she never had before. 'Please, Tom,' she panted, reaching into her top drawer and strewing foil packets all over the bed.

When she turned back, Tom was kneeling at the bottom of her bed. Pushing her legs apart, he eased between them, his head descending towards the juncture of her thighs. 'No.' She half sat up. 'I want you...'

His tongue lazily lapped at the most sensitive part of her and she fell back with a long, low moan. 'You want...?'

'That,' she whispered. 'I want that.'

That clever tongue sampled and circled, tested and teased. One strong finger slid inside her, pressing against something that had her clutching the bedsheets. Heat and pleasure gathered and receded…gathered and receded…as if he was playing some game with her body until she was almost sobbing. 'Tom,' she panted, *please.*

Mouth, tongue and fingers all became firmer, more assured, and her body lifted as she clapped a hand over her mouth to smother her cries as pleasure exploded and flung her outside of herself. As she floated back down she couldn't recall ever feeling so peaceful, so right. Opening her eyes, she found Tom smiling down at her. There was nothing smug in his grin, just delight. It made her breath catch. 'That was really something.'

'Something good, I hope.'

'Something splendidly and fabulously and brilliantly excellent.' She nodded and he rolled on a condom. She shook herself. 'Oh, let me return the favour. I—'

'Charlie.' His hands went either side of her head, making her subside back to the mattress. 'I have plans for you. I'm not going to be satisfied if you don't come at least two, maybe three times tonight.'

She swallowed, unable to find her voice.

'Do you have a problem with that?'

She shook her head. No problem at all.

The thick length of him nudged against her entrance and she angled her hips, and when he slid inside her, her fingers at his waist tightened and she gasped.

He immediately stilled. 'Did I hurt you?'

She shook her head. Tom King was built along very generous lines, but he hadn't hurt her. 'You feel *perfect*.'

A gentle hand brushed the hair from her face. 'That's the nicest compliment I've ever received.'

Their gazes connected and something sweet and deep arced between them. A kernel of unease unfurled inside her. 'This doesn't mean anything, Tom. We're just messing about.'

He nodded as if he had taken that for granted, and she felt herself turn red. He winked down at her. 'But I'm of the opinion that if we're messing about, we might as well do it properly. In fact, we might as well excel at messing about.'

Her embarrassment faded and she found herself chuckling. 'What an excellent idea.'

And then he moved inside her and her entire body came alive again—awake and hungry. Her hands explored the hard planes of his back and the firm flesh of his buttocks, glorying in their power and beauty—and all the while the pleasure built and built until she wrapped her legs around his waist and pressed her face into his shoulder, her entire body contracting as another orgasm hit her—wave upon wave of pleasure washing through her. And then that big masculine body stiffened and shuddered, and she slid her arms around his chest and held him as he too came with an intensity that went on and on and on.

* * *

The alarm jangled Charlie awake and she had to force herself up through a thick fog, her hand fumbling, to turn it off. What on earth…? She felt as if she'd been hit by a truck and caressed all over with feathers both at the same time.

She bolted upright in bed. Oh, God! She and Tom had… *Several times.*

True to his word, she'd come three times. And while she might feel heavy with sleep, her body hummed with the kind of happy harmony that only a good orgasm, or three, could give.

'You going to hear angelic choirs next?' she muttered, throwing the bedclothes back, pulling on her fluffy camouflage robe and striding across to open the curtains and flood the room with early-morning sunlight.

She needed to shine that same bright light on the events of the previous night, and not make the mistake of seeing them through a romantic, soft-focus haze. Because that way danger lay. Last night had been amazing, but… She chafed her arms against a sudden chill. She was *not* falling in love with Tom.

Scratching a hand through her hair, she tried to get her mind around it all. Sparks had flown between her and Tom from the moment she'd brought him that beer at Eliza's ball—the long, lingering looks since then, the near kisses, the fantasising—but she'd never meant to act on them.

Except his understanding last night, his generosity of spirit, had undone her. Utterly. She rubbed both hands over her face. But falling into bed with him? Really? Reckless and foolish, much?

Breathe, Charlie, breathe.

Her heart pounded and she had to brace her hands on her knees. She would *not* fall in love with Tom. She was *not* falling in love with another man who'd leave her for the city. When Connor had walked away, she'd never felt so lost and alone—not even that time when she was thirteen and had fallen off her horse and broken her arm, two hours from home.

Her horse, spooked by a snake, had bucked and bolted—leaving her bruised and stunned on the ground. She'd had to fight nausea and the impending threat of losing consciousness to keep her wits and make for a landmark her mother and Pop would head to as soon as they realised she was missing. She'd waited there praying they'd find her sooner rather than later. They had. But it had felt like the longest, loneliest day of her life.

Until Connor. Ten years together and a whole life mapped out, and he hadn't even had the decency to break up with her face-to-face. He'd turned her world upside-down in the worst possible way, and she had no intention of going through something like that again.

Grabbing her toiletry bag, she headed for the bathroom. A bracing cold shower would get her brain working again, help her find her common sense and—

'Good morning.'

She came to a dead halt. Tom sat on the sofa. Grey eyes made a lazy perusal that left her tingling all over. Her fingers clutched her robe at the throat. 'Good morning.'

His eyes immediately narrowed. 'Having regrets?'

Her heart gave a funny kick. Last night this man had found out that she'd been lying to him and he'd forgiven her—not just forgiven her, but had immediately taken her side, appalled at his father's actions. He didn't deserve her stiffness or awkwardness. 'Not regrets, no.'

She moved to the seat opposite and perched on the edge. Did her best not to notice that *he* didn't look sleep deprived. He looked vibrant, literally glowing with good health, as if he was ready to take on the world.

'Then what's bugging you?'

She stared at her hands. It was too hard to think straight when she looked at Tom. 'I'm shocked at the way I behaved.' She hauled in a breath. '*I* kissed you. *I* said I didn't want to stop. I practically dragged you into my bedroom.'

'You think I was a passive actor?'

It was nearly impossible to resist his grin. Her lips twitched. 'Not passive, no, but…' She shook her head. 'I behaved recklessly last night, Tom.

And in the cold light of day I can't help feeling it wasn't wise.'

Something inside of him snapped closed, and she called herself every kind of a fool for mourning the fact that she no longer had access to it. 'I see.'

'For a start, I have a grudge against your father. I want to right a wrong.'

'And you think I'll interfere with that?'

'No.' She wrinkled her nose. 'But it does complicate things. It could be construed as me trying to manipulate you. I… *That's* not what happened!' Oh God, would he now think…? 'I wasn't trying to deflect your attention—'

'I didn't think that for a moment, Charlie.'

Okay. Good. She let out a breath. 'What happened last night…'

'I'm listening,' he said when she hesitated.

'It was extraordinary…amazing.' Their gazes caught and held. 'But it was also raw and intense.' She moistened suddenly dry lips. 'Sometimes that means something—and sometimes it doesn't—but it makes me wary. It makes me think last night should be a one-off, not-to-be-repeated event.'

His lips twisted and heat flooded her cheeks. 'I'm not saying you wanted a repeat performance, I just…' She snapped her mouth shut. She'd dug a big enough hole for herself already.

Tom scratched both hands through his hair, the shrug he gave too casual. 'You had an itch that needed scratching, and now that it's been scratched...'

'Damn it, Tom! I'm not falling in love with another city boy—got it? This whole situation—me looking after your little girl, living under your roof and seeing you every day, and acting like a kind of family—it has the potential to...'

'To...?'

'Look, you're hot and a seriously excellent lover, and I like you as a person; Bea is funny and quirky and adorable; and look at how you live—it's on a whole other level from most people. This—me being Bea's nanny—is a temporary arrangement. I can't afford to let it go to my head. I don't want to get too used to it. I don't want to start thinking I matter more to the two of you than I do. I *don't* want to feel lost and alone when it all comes to an end.'

He stared at her as if at a loss for what to say.

'This is not about me using you and then casting you aside. It's about me protecting myself.'

'I'm sorry.' Reaching across, he took her hands in his and something in his touch gentled the agitated pounding of her heart. 'I'm sorry,' he repeated. 'I'm being graceless in my disappointment.'

In his...?

'I was hoping we could continue our *messing about*, but this situation *is* temporary.' He said it as if warning her. 'Once it comes to an end there won't be anything more on offer. I'll fly back to Sydney with Bea…'

'And I'll ride off into the sunset with Cranky Frank, Lady Trippy and my pack of kelpies.'

'I liked messing about with you, Charlie. But I don't want to hurt you. I like you too much to do something like that.'

'Thank you.'

He nodded, all business once again. 'So a once-off never-to-be-repeated event it is.'

He released her hands and she moistened her lips, nodded, wondering why she didn't feel happier about the way this had all played out. 'Well, now that we have that sorted, I'll grab a shower.'

Charlie moved to the bathroom, her usual fizzy bounciness nowhere to be seen. Was that due to a lack of sleep? Or the conversation they'd just had?

Tom's heart gave a sickening kick. He should've behaved better just then. What the hell was wrong with him? Acting all hurt and cast aside when she'd made it clear that the events of the previous evening wouldn't be repeated. As if he were an over-eager, naïve teenager who built dreams from fairy-floss nothings.

Last night *had* been extraordinary, Charlie had been right about that, but it didn't mean anything. Marrying Madeline had taught him the dangers of reading too much into physical encounters—the foolishness of latching on to tempting distractions when his life was a mess. He'd confused temporary respite and comfort with something deep and permanent—with something that would last. He wouldn't make the same mistake again. He wasn't *failing* again.

When it had become apparent that Madeline hadn't loved him—that what she'd loved was the life she could have with him—his marriage had become a prison. It had been even more confronting to find his love for her draining away as if it had never been. The entire episode had left him empty, disillusioned, and ashamed. A failure.

The thought of one day glancing up and catching disappointment, disenchantment, dissatisfaction in another woman's face and knowing he was the cause of it? His stomach gave a sickening roll. No matter how attractive he found Charlie, he wasn't going through any of that again.

His phone vibrated in his pocket. Glancing at it, his jaw dropped. *Holy guacamole!* He pressed it to his ear. 'Jack!'

'I have eleven unanswered calls from you, Tom. That's overboard, even for you. What's so damn important?'

His brows shot up. 'You're seriously asking that after Fraser's bombshell?'

Jack remained disturbingly silent. Not for the first time he had to ask himself if it *had* been a bombshell for Jack?

His hand tightened about the phone. When Madeline had died, Jack had organised a month's worth of dinner deliveries for Tom and Bea. It had been a nice thing to do—thoughtful, practical. The brotherly bond might be frail and flimsy, but it was still there, buried beneath everything else.

'Logan, Fitz and I are going to fight it.' He lumped Fitz in with him and Logan even though he hadn't had a chance to talk to his younger brother yet. 'I want to know if you're with us or against us.'

Again Jack remained silent. Because he was shocked Tom was questioning his loyalties? Or because he was plotting to burn Kings Reach to the ground? Tom wished he knew. 'In the meantime, I'm trying to talk sense into Dad before it becomes a full-scale war, which is going about as well as you'd expect. Fraser and I have always been oil and water.'

'Not always.'

The time before Will's death rose in his mind. There *had* been times when he and his father had managed to find a strange kind of peace with one another. If Jack could remember the good times…

'Jack, you're the only one of us who's ever had any real influence with Dad. I—'

'I've no plans to return to Kings Reach any time soon, Tom. I've a lot on my plate and—'

'Running away might be your MO, Jack, but what makes you think your pain is more important than everyone else's?'

The words flew out of him like buckshot. 'You weren't here to witness Mum's descent into grief—a grief your absence added to. You weren't here to see Logan throwing himself into his studies or see Fitz become a damn zombie for months on end.'

'Tom, I—'

'*No!*' He didn't know where the anger had come from—but now that the dam had been loosened he couldn't contain it. 'You *weren't* here when we needed you. I know you were only seventeen when you left, and none of us makes good decisions when we're seventeen, but you have the chance to do the right thing now. Do it!'

But he was talking to thin air. Jack had ended the call. Fighting an urge to kick a chair, he turned to find Charlie in the bathroom doorway, smelling like a vanilla cupcake. Wide eyes surveyed him with shock and…sympathy? His throat tightened. He should've taken Jack's call out on the balcony. Movement sounded from Bea's bedroom.

'I'll look after Bea while you…'

He raised an eyebrow.

'Grab a shower and—' she gestured at him '—make yourself look human.'

It was the way she said it, though. Sure, there was sympathy and it ought to have chafed, but there was also a twinkle, as if she was figuratively throwing up her hands, rolling her eyes and groaning 'Family, huh? Can't live with them, can't live without them'. It had an unexpected laugh huffing out of him. What was it about this woman that reminded him that humour and laughter existed alongside frustration and disappointment?

Braced beneath jets of hot water a short time later, steam rising up all around him, his mind wandered to what it would've been like if Charlie hadn't vetoed any more messing around. To being able to pull her into the shower with him and soaping that delectable body with his hands and letting them roam…

With a curse he turned the hot tap off, hissing when freezing cold water hit overheated flesh. He wasn't building another prison for himself; and he wouldn't do anything to hurt Charlie either. *That* would be unforgivable.

That night, after Bea had been put to bed, Tom found Charlie outside on the balcony. Rather than her PJs and camouflage robe, she wore jeans and jumper. To prevent things from becoming accidentally hot and heavy between them?

She sat on the bench, her feet on the railing, and her head tipped back to stare at the stars. The night air was chilly and she had a blanket draped over her legs.

He glanced up at the sky too and a breath eased out of him.

'It's something, isn't it?' she murmured.

She could say that again. 'I've been forgetting to look up.'

'Well—' her eyes remained on the sky '—sometimes it's important to keep your gaze trained on the path at your feet. But you should find the time to look up once in a while.' She glanced over. 'Though I expect you can't really see the stars in the city.'

Did she mention the city to remind them both of the gulf that lay between them? He forced his gaze back to the sky, fighting a frown. Who the hell was the city boy that had broken her heart? That Connor she'd mentioned?

'Are you okay, Tom?'

She shuffled along the bench in a silent invitation for him to sit and he appreciated her low-key manner. He also appreciated that she didn't pretend that she hadn't overheard his phone call with Jack this morning. He knew that if he said everything was fine, she'd let it drop.

He sat. 'Hard to say. I'm good with my kid and that's the most important thing. I'm good with my work—also important, as it puts a roof over our heads and food on the table and continues to provide me with a mental challenge.'

'So life is more good than bad.'

He eased back. With a single sentence, Charlie had him reframing not only the situation at Kings Reach, but his entire life too. He and Bea had a *good* life—an enviable life. Bea also now had another uncle firmly in her corner—an uncle who adored her and one she now trusted. He'd like to strengthen that bond further, but a start had been made—a good strong start.

Regardless of what happened with the station,

none of that would change. He and Bea had their health and so did his brothers. So did his father. He might not always like the man or the decisions he made, but the thought of his father sick or dying twisted something inside him out of shape.

'Life is more good than bad,' he agreed.

'I've been sitting out here reminding myself of that too.'

He glanced across. 'Are you worried about Melaleuca Downs's future?' He would *not* let his father destroy the station.

She rolled her eyes. 'Show me a station owner who doesn't worry about that.'

'Fair point.' He did his best not to focus on the perfection of her profile.

'I've been reminding myself that even if I can't force Fraser to honour his side of the contract, that if we work hard—and if nothing else goes wrong—we'll pull ourselves back from the brink. As long as we double down and stay focused we should be fine.'

As long as nothing else went wrong. The thought of Charlie and her family suffering hardship because of his father chafed at him. He pulled in a breath. 'I've been thinking… If we join forces, we can help each other.'

Her gaze remained trained on the sky. 'How?'

'What I'm about to tell you is in the strictest confidence.'

That had her turning to face him. 'Okay.'

'When my father dies, Kings Reach is supposed to be inherited by me and my brothers equally. An irrevocable trust was created after my mother died—at her behest. It means each of us gets an equal share and an equal say in the future of the station.'

'Which is as it should be.'

Things inside him went hard and cold. 'On the night of the ball, my father announced that he was making a move to break the trust.'

Charlie's feet hit the floor. 'Change it *how*?'

'We'll all still inherit an equal share financially, but in his new will Fraser plans to give Jack full management of Kings Reach. Jack would have the sole right to make all business decisions for the station. The rest of us wouldn't get a say.'

She frowned. Her frown became a scowl. '*Why* would he do such a thing?'

Her outrage warmed some of the cold places inside of him. 'In Fraser's eyes, none of us has ever lived up to the legend that is Jack.'

Behind the blue of her eyes, her mind worked. 'So all of Fitz's hard work on the ecotourism side of things…?'

'Jack could wipe that off the face of the earth with a single wave of his hand.'

CHAPTER EIGHT

CHARLIE TRIED TO make sense of what Tom had just told her. 'He could turn your home into a luxury hotel.' Everyone knew Jack had made a name for himself on the international stage doing exactly that.

'Yep.'

Her heart knocked against her ribs. 'He could overstock the station—bringing in more cattle when the rest of us landowners are trying to find a happy balance between herd sizes and environmental sustainability.'

'He could turn the whole damn station into a pineapple farm if he wanted.'

'He wouldn't be that stupid!' He mightn't have lived in the Kimberley for twenty years, but he wouldn't make a daft decision like that.

'That's not the point, Charlie. The fact is if Jack took such a freak notion into his head...'

'He'd have the power to enforce it.' She rubbed a hand over her face. 'He could sell mining rights, lease the land to whoever he wanted.'

'He could *sell* the station.'

Her stomach scrunched up tight. Would Jack do that to his brothers? She went to ask, recalled the overheard phone conversation, and bit the question back. Things were tense between Tom and Jack. That meant they were probably tense between Jack and the rest of his brothers too.

Why would Fraser…?

Damn him to hell! What a terrible thing to do to his three younger sons. If Pop and Mum cut her out of the line of inheritance it'd devastate her.

She fought an urge to plant herself in Tom's lap and hug him. What Fraser had done to Melaleuca seemed trivial compared to what he was doing to his own family. Tom might look composed and stoic, but underneath he had to be a mass of hurt. 'You have any idea why he's being such a bonehead?'

One corner of his mouth hooked up. She might not be able to hug him, but the fact she could still make him smile had her chest loosening. He shook his head. 'No.'

'Can he do it? Can he break the trust?'

'Logan says not.'

Logan was a lawyer. He'd know.

'But that won't stop him from trying.'

And until this was resolved, Tom, Fitz and Logan would feel as if they were treading water. What a mess. 'What can I do to help?'

The stars in the sky were reflected in his eyes, and a hard longing had the breath jamming in her lungs. This man with his strong jaw and broad shoulders, his resolution to do what was right rather than easy, sent a deep, hard yearning through her. She wanted him so much it hurt.

'You offer to help without knowing what I plan to ask of you?'

'What Fraser is doing is wrong.' And last night Tom had stood by her—he'd stood by *her*. 'So yes.'

'The fact you don't like Fraser has nothing to do with it, I suppose?'

Actually, it didn't, which made no sense. But it made enough sense to frighten her. She needed to lighten things up before…

Before what?

Before she did or said something stupid, that was what. She tossed her hair back and held her thumb and forefinger an inch apart. 'Perhaps a little.'

His lips twitched, but he sobered again. 'I've remained at the station to try and talk sense into Fraser—make him see what a bad decision this is—to convince him to give it up.' Firm lips twisted. 'That's gone as well as you'd expect.'

Which didn't surprise her.

'But since discovering that he reneged on your contract…'

He rose to pace. Long legs. Firm buttocks encased in worn denim. The sinuous shift of his body. A pulse bloomed to life at the centre of her and her fingers curled into her palms. Had she left marks on Tom's body? When they'd made love had she—?

'My father and I have a difficult relationship,' he began.

She shook herself.

'And yet I'd have bet everything I owned that he'd never dishonour a contract or go back on his word. His reputation means everything to him.'

Tom would've lost everything on that bet. A part of her wished she hadn't told him—that he could have kept his illusions.

'And now I'm wondering how many other contracts he's dishonoured.'

She moistened her lips. 'Fraser might be the most powerful landholder in the Kimberley, but not even he could prevent the whispers and gossip if he'd been making a habit of it.' She stood too. 'Word *would* get around.'

'How do you know? *Your* family have kept quiet. Others might've kept quiet out of fear of reprisal too.'

Her stomach churned.

'If I can get proof that Fraser has been taking advantage of his position and not honouring contracts, then I can use it against him.'

She plonked back on the bench, her mind awhirl.

'I could confront him with it like you planned to, threaten to make it public unless he drops his legal action to break the trust. If he still refuses, I'll pass the information on to Logan and we'll use it in the case we're building against him. I'll also personally fund each instance of a dishonoured contract.'

She stared at him, speechless.

He sat too, reached for her hand. 'I know these are ugly tactics, Charlie, but…'

'But sometimes you have to fight fire with fire.' Which happened to be a literal land-management tactic out here in the Kimberley. During the early dry season, landholders would set a series of cool burns to prevent large, destructive wildfires from occurring later in the season when the scrub and grasses were parched and arid, before the massive lightning storms that presaged the beginning of the wet season hit.

Out here wildfires could be devastating—burning thousands of hectares and killing everything in their path, including cattle, crops, homes and people. Tom wanted to set a controlled burn before things got out of hand with Fraser—before too many people were hurt. She found herself totally on board with that. 'So we need to gather information. How do you propose we set about doing that?'

'First of all I want to find out if there's more to the disagreements between Fraser and your mother than either of us have ever been told. I need to discover why Fraser would want to hurt your family.' She stared, her mind racing.

'The family name means everything to him.'

She swallowed. More than his sons?

'He'll do anything to protect it. If I can show him the potential damage a court case could do to the King name…' Everything about him sharpened. 'We need to visit my godfather, Elliot Rawal. He knows a lot about my family and the families of the region.'

Her jaw dropped. 'Elliot Rawal, the artist?'

He nodded.

'No way! Your godfather is *Elliot Rawal*?'

He grinned and her heart thump-thumped. 'The godparents are a veritable who's-who of notable Australians. Jack's godfather is Angus Stuart, the former state premier; Logan's godmother is Margaret Li, the high-court judge; and Fitz's godfather is Julius Martisson, the Olympic rowing medallist.'

She gaped at him. She couldn't help it. 'My godparents are my Uncle Wayne and Auntie Linda,' she heard herself say.

'Angus and Margaret were at uni with Dad. While Elliot and Julius went to uni with Mum. Our parents wanted us to have *every advantage*.'

Her mum had just wanted her to be loved.

'They've all kept in touch with us.'

'Where does your godfather live?'

'Melbourne.' He leaned back against the bench. 'Tomorrow, Charlie, we're going to Melbourne.'

She did her best to take this announcement in her stride. 'Right, I'd best go pack bags for me and Bea, then.'

'No.'

She'd started to rise, but lowered herself back to the bench to stare at the lean finger he tapped against his lips. She recalled the way that finger had traced a path of fire down her body…

'We'll leave the day after tomorrow, and don't pack for Bea. I'll ask Fitz to babysit while we're gone.'

'Tom, that's what you're paying *me* for.'

Resting elbows on his knees, he stared out at the night. 'One of the things I want to achieve while I'm at Kings Reach is to cement the relationship between Fitz and Bea.'

'You've achieved that—they adore one another.'

'It's been started, but I want their relationship embedded like the roots of a river gum.' One of his hands clenched. 'I want it strong and solid and resilient.'

She rubbed a hand over her chest. 'Have you recently received bad news on the health front or something?'

His smile when it came made her stupid heart pitter-patter. 'I'm healthy as a horse. But Will, Mum, Madeline, they all made me realise life can change in an instant. My motto these days is to pray for the best, but plan for the worst.'

His words had a burn stretching through her chest. Losing his wife must've been the most dreadful thing. What had she been like—the woman who'd managed to capture this man's heart?

'Doing the practical things that a full day of childcare requires, rather than just the fun things like playing with puppies…it's different. I want Bea and Fitz to negotiate that at least once so…'

'So they know how to do it again if they ever have to.'

'Exactly.' He sent her a sidelong glance. 'You don't have to come to Melbourne if you don't want to, Charlie. I know the city holds no charms for you. I can do this on my own. But if you stay, both Bea and Fitz will lean on you.'

'Which defeats the purpose.' She fought a frown. 'But Melbourne is a bit of a hike, Tom. It probably means two nights away rather than one.'

He nodded. 'Fitz will have Mrs McRae and Annalise to help. I'm not abandoning him to flounder on his own. If Logan can work it out— and he did—then Fitz will too.'

She ached that he felt this a necessary measure—putting steps in place in case he shouldn't be here in the future. But it warmed her to the soles of her feet that he'd go to such lengths to ensure Bea would be looked after.

Reaching across, he squeezed her hand. 'I'll be asking questions about *your* family. I want to find out if Fraser has a grudge against them, some imagined score to settle. It's only right that you're there when I ask them. Fraser's actions have put *your* home in jeopardy.'

Her chest gave a silly flutter of excitement. 'Okay. I guess we're going to Melbourne.'

Their eyes caught and held and the memory of their lovemaking rose up around them. Tom's thumb caressed the inside of her wrist. His breathing grew unsteady. So did hers. It'd be so easy to press her lips to his; to throw caution to the wind and indulge in a hot and heavy fling. It'd be heady and glorious and—

What about when he leaves and returns to the city? Do you think it'll be glorious then?

The thought had her going cold all over. She removed her hand from his, and eased away.

Tom's jaw clenched, but he nodded. 'I'm sorry a city boy broke your heart, Charlie.'

She gave a what-can-you-do shrug, but the remembered pain and loss, the feeling of having had to start her life from scratch, all the dreams that had died when Connor had walked away, hit her again now. She *wasn't* going through that a second time.

Tom might be hot, and he might be utterly lovely, but he wasn't staying. She'd be nothing more than a brief fling. Some instinct she refused to ignore warned her that wouldn't be enough.

She had it within her power to protect her own heart, and she wasn't handing those reins to anyone else. She rose. 'Time for me to turn in. Night, Tom.'

'Night, Charlie.'

Tom had booked them into the swankiest hotel Charlie had ever seen. The foyer looked like something out of a movie set. Men and women in stylish suits and designer labels sipped cocktails at the bar or sipped lattes at the cafe—beautiful places for meeting with friends.

She drifted across to a series of bewitching window displays from a row of boutiques while Tom checked them in. Designer jewellery, chic accessories and high-end fashion provided a feast for the eyes. Reaching out, she brushed her fingers across the silk of a dress in tones of jewelled blues and dusky pinks—gorgeous! She stepped back, though, when she spied the price tag. Yikes!

'Anything take your fancy?'

Tom's breath disturbed the hair at her nape when he bent down to see what had caught her eye, making her shiver.

He gestured to the dress. 'That would look great on you.'

Perhaps, but at that price? No way. She turned her back resolutely on the display. 'All checked in?'

He held up a plastic key and led them to the bank of lifts.

Minutes later she found herself standing at an enormous window, gaping at the jaw-dropping views over the Yarra River and the cityscape that lay before them. 'A penthouse? You booked us a two-bedroom penthouse suite?'

He spread his hands, his mouth hooking up. 'Why, you don't like it?'

* * *

Tom watched myriad emotions flit across Charlie's face. Charlie's very attractive face. Not that he was paying attention to that, remember?

It shouldn't be this hard, though.

'You could've booked me into the budget hotel across the road.'

What the…? *'No.'*

Her head jerked back at his fierceness.

'I always stay here when I'm in Melbourne. When they're working, my staff stay here on my tab. And as my guest, you'll stay here too.' He folded his arms. 'Do you think you're a second-class citizen or something—that you should be banished to the attics and the servants' quarters?'

'Of course not. It's just… This must be costing you a fortune.'

He blinked. He wasn't used to people caring how much money he spent. 'Making money comes easily to me. My superpower if you will. You might as well settle in and enjoy this. I plan to.'

She glanced around, fidgeted. 'I don't think I brought the right clothes.'

'We can buy you new ones. We're in the city. Here there are plenty of shops.'

Her eyes flashed. 'Spend good money on clothes I'll only wear once? Not going to happen!'

Her outrage made him smile, lightened some tiny piece of heaviness in his chest. Madeline would've jumped at the chance to go shopping, but not Charlie apparently.

'I packed a classic little black dress for dinner with your godfather. For the rest of the time I'll make do with my jeans.'

'Sounds perfect. And speaking of Elliot, we need to come up with a gameplan.' He crossed to the minibar. 'Want a drink?'

He needed to start focusing on the right things. Rather than the way he wanted to ravage Charlie's lips whenever she smiled, or how he ached to bury his face in her hair whenever she lifted it off her nape.

She moved across to study the offerings, dredging him in her scent. *Not helping.* She eventually selected a complimentary bottle of water. Hmm, she hadn't got the hang of relaxing into all of this luxury yet, had she? Snagging a juice, he joined her on the enormous sofa.

'Why do we need a gameplan? He's your godfather—won't he just tell you what he knows?'

'Look, Elliot is a great guy, but you have to play by the rules. So I've booked him a room here for the night and we have a dinner reservation at one of the hottest restaurants in the city. They're usually booked out months in advance.'

'Usually?'

'I pulled some strings.'

'Elliot must have money and influence of his own, though.'

'Of course he does. But it's so much sweeter when someone else picks up the bill.'

She rolled her eyes. 'It all sounds like a lot of nonsense to me. So we wine and dine him…and then?'

'I'll idly slip into the conversation that I have an excellent investment prospect for him *and* that I have tickets for the big football match on the weekend that I'm not sure if I'll now be able to attend…'

'We're buttering him up?'

'And once we've done that, we can ask our questions.'

'And hope he answers them.'

'He'll answer them.' He had no doubt of that.

Her hands twisted together. 'What's my role in all of this, Tom? Am I supposed to sit there and smile prettily?'

'I just want you to be yourself. Relax and enjoy the evening, Charlie. Elliot is going to love you.'

Elliot was already seated when they arrived at the restaurant. The two men shook hands and then Tom gestured to Charlie. 'This is my friend Charlie Ashwell, who just happens to be a great art lover.' Charlie swung back to him with wide eyes and he grinned. 'What? You didn't think I'd noticed the way you study the paintings at Kings Reach?' He held her chair out for her, and they all sat.

Elliot leaned towards her. 'Have you seen the Namatjira?'

She swooned. 'It's breathtaking.'

'If you can, try and catch a glimpse of the Nolan in Fraser's office.'

Elliot lapped up the excellent food, the fine wine, and the attention with a flattering relish. He put Charlie at ease, relating scandalous stories about the art world until she clapped a hand over her mouth to muffle her laughter. She looked stunning in her *classic little black dress*. The sweetheart neckline, while modest, still hinted at the dusky shadow of her cleavage, while the above-knee hemline showcased the perfection of her legs. Things inside him clenched and un-clenched…and craved.

She didn't relax enough to order much for dinner, though. She'd taken one look at the prices and raised scandalised eyes to Tom's before slapping the menu closed and ordering a salad. *A salad!* She'd then declined dessert, but at least she'd agreed to a coffee while the two men lingered over their brandies.

'So, dear boy, now that you've given me the sweeties, want to tell me why you really wanted to see me?'

Tom grinned. 'It's good to see you too, Elliot.'

Elliot chuckled and slapped him on the shoulder.

'We're after information, and that's your speciality.' He paused. 'I want to know if there's anything to the falling-out between Fraser and Victoria Ashwell all those years ago—was there anything dire?'

Elliot's gaze swung to Charlie, immediately making the connection. 'You're Vicky's girl.'

'That's me.'

'You youngsters are taking me back now. Fraser and Vicky were fast friends back in the day. Fraser treated her like the little sister he'd never had, but they fell out over the lowlife loser she married. Sorry, dear, I suspect that lowlife loser is your father.'

'You're not a bit sorry, you old rogue,' she shot back, her lips twitching. 'You're just lucky that in this instance I happen to agree with you.'

Elliot winked. 'I thought you might. But other than that...' He shook his head. 'I can't recall that there's been any real bad blood between them. I mean, there have been a few minor skirmishes over contracts they've both tendered for over the years, but nothing major.'

'So there's no reason why my father would wish the Ashwells ill?'

'No, my dear boy, absolutely not.'

'No vendettas?' Charlie checked. 'No issues with my grandfather?'

'With Sidney? Heck no. Sid kept himself well and truly out of it. I suspect he and Fraser were as one on the subject of your father.' Elliot glanced at Charlie and then Tom. 'I did a bit of digging after we arranged to meet up—hoping to find out what would bring you all this way to see me. I uncovered nothing.'

Charlie frowned. 'How can you know so much when you live so far away?'

Elliot touched a finger to the side of his nose. 'It's who you know, my dear. My brother-in-law owns the major trucking company that services the Kimberley and the Northern Territory.'

Charlie choked on her coffee.

'And let's just say he hears…things. Then there's Janice, the former Federal Member for the Kimberley. We courted for a while back in the day. I met her when visiting Fraser during the Ord Valley Muster. Fun times. Janice does a bit of contract work now for the Agricultural Board. And then there's the other godparents. Between us, our reach is broad. It's extraordinary what we can find out.'

'And yet, in this instance,' Tom said, 'you found nothing of note?'

Elliot's gaze slid to his brandy. 'Like?'

Tom couldn't work out if Elliot was being evasive or fishing for information. 'Like Fraser signing contracts and then reneging on them.'

'God, no!' Elliot's brandy hit the table with a thump. He glared at Tom. 'Your father is a complicated man, but he's a man of his word.'

So why did he feel that Elliot wasn't telling him everything?

'We're no further ahead than we were before we left.' Charlie thumped down to the sofa.

Tom wished he'd been able to find a clue for her. For them. 'Elliot has a lot of contacts, but he's not infallible, Charlie. I'll put out feelers when we're back home.'

He sat too, studied her for a moment. She brushed the hair off her face. 'What?'

'Are you feeling okay? You didn't eat much tonight.'

'Wasn't hungry. All of that travelling, I suppose.'

Hmm… 'A shame. The food was good.' He stretched out his legs, let his head drop back. 'If you could choose a last meal, what would you have?'

She'd stretched back too. 'Your meal was *that* good?'

He shook his head. 'I'd choose a steak—a Kimberley Red—fine-textured with a deep flavour. Nothing can beat that.'

'Steak is the one thing not lacking on the menu at home. I'd have Sydney rock oysters. I've only had them once, but they were the best things I've ever eaten.'

'I'd have mussels for a starter.'

'I've never tried them. Good?'

He nodded. 'You?'

'A couple of king prawns, I think.'

'You're going hard on the seafood there, Charlie.'

She shrugged. He tried not to notice how her dress had ridden up slightly, revealing more of her luscious thighs. 'We don't have it much at home. I'm adding a salad into the mix to cover all the food groups, and some gorgeous artisan-style bread to round things off.'

'And dessert?'

'Sticky toffee pudding with butterscotch sauce.'

'Hell, yeah, sign me up for that too.'

Their gazes caught and held. For the briefest of moments he saw his own hunger reflected back at him, but then Charlie rose. 'I'm turning in. Goodnight, Tom.'

Gritting his teeth and clenching his hands, he remained exactly where he was.

The next morning, they breakfasted in the hotel's dining room—a safer option than having it delivered to their suite. He needed the buffer of other people to prevent him from doing something stupid. 'Is there anything you'd like to do today?'

'Nope, so if you wanted to head back to Kings Reach, we could probably get flights out this afternoon.'

'I'd prefer not to. I spoke to Fitz earlier. He and Bea are managing splendidly.' He leaned towards her, not giving her time to object. 'And I feel duty bound to prove to you that the city does have some compensations.'

Her lips twitched. 'You trying to convert me to a city girl, Tom?'

'Let's just say I'm broadening your horizons.'

They spent the morning at the city's gallery.

He let her gaze at beautiful art until she'd had her fill. 'It's amazing,' she kept murmuring in an undertone, 'all amazing.'

As they emerged back into the sunshine she lifted her hands and let them drop. 'Okay, I'll concede that access to great art is a major compensation.'

Those blue eyes were alive with curiosity and interest—staring at the bustling city in front of them as if trying to take it all in. It fired things to life inside him. Things that had been sadly lacking in recent years—like a sense of novelty and wonder, and the feeling of being deeply alive.

He rubbed his hands together. 'Buckle up, we've only just started.'

For lunch they ate dumplings in Chinatown. He then took her to Old Melbourne Gaol—spooky, unsettling and full of history—hoping it would appeal to her sense of quirk. It did. And then followed it up with a visit to the State Library a block away—one of the most beautiful buildings in the city. They made their way back to the hotel, window shopping along the way.

'Oh, Tom, that was the most wonderful day. Thank you!'

The smile she sent him had Tom fumbling with their room key. He wrestled the door open. 'The day's not over yet.' Then he handed the room key to her. 'I need to go back out, but I'll collect you at seven for dinner.'

Her face fell. 'But...'

He waited. When she didn't add anything, he shrugged. 'You've time to take a stroll along the river if you want, to have a nap…or a long bath. The minibar is at your disposal, and don't hesitate to order anything from Room Service. I'll see you in a couple of hours.' Lifting his hand in a wave, he turned on his heel and left.

Charlie wouldn't do anything as frivolous as ordering room service. She probably wouldn't even help herself to a juice. If Charlie wouldn't come to the party, he'd just have to bring the party to her.

CHAPTER NINE

CHARLIE STARTED AT the knock on the door.

Opening it, she found a member of the housekeeping staff holding a long cardboard box out to her, embossed with the label of one of the downstairs boutiques. 'For you, Ms Ashwell.'

Charlie took it automatically. 'I… Thank you.'

There had to be some mistake. She hadn't ordered anything. Setting it on the table, she planted her hands on her hips and stared at it. It might be a mistake, but…where was the harm in taking the tiniest of peeks? She'd be oh-so-careful.

Opening the lid—*carefully*—she lifted out layers of tissue paper to discover the dress she'd admired yesterday. The sapphire-blues and dusky pinks made her swoon. She reached out to touch it, but pulled her hand back at the last moment. The dress wasn't hers. There had obviously been some kind of mix-up.

A frivolous part of her wished she'd bought it yesterday. Then it *would* be hers.

Nonsense. Her money was better spent saving her home from imminent disaster. She had started to replace the tissue paper when she spied an envelope that had slipped down the side of the box—an envelope addressed to her. The enclosed card read:

Charlie, after seeing you gaze at this so longingly yesterday, I couldn't resist buying it for you.

Her pulse set off at a gallop. Tom!

The dress was made for you.

He'd bought her the dress? The jolt of euphoria became an erratic, discordant trot that made her feel queasy.

You're going to think this is about the sex—a thank-you, some kind of kiss-off, or an attempt to seduce you.

She sucked her bottom lip into her mouth. Apparently she was transparent.

It's not about the sex, Charlie. You've been so careful not to take advantage of my money, have been too frugal, if you want the truth, and it got my back up.

It…what?

It's made me determined to force you to indulge—just once.

What did that mean?

Obviously, I'm not going to force you. You don't have to accept the dress, though I very much hope you will. I hope you'll wear it to dinner tonight. You don't have to join me for dinner either if you'd rather not. Though I very much hope you'll choose to.

Very had been underlined. She bit her lip. The thing was, she wanted to. *Very* much. And that sent alarm bells ringing through her. She liked Tom. If she wasn't careful she'd be in danger of liking him too much.

She drifted across to the window to stare at the city spread before her. Tom had made it perfectly clear that he wasn't interested in anything long-term. She couldn't afford to get too hung up on him. His stay in the Kimberley was temporary. If she gave in to temptation and had a fling with him, he'd still leave. And she'd be left behind.

The thought of being abandoned by Tom in the same way Connor had abandoned her… Her heart lodged in her throat, stretching it into a painful ache. She wasn't giving any man a chance to treat her like that again. It had taken her too long to rebuild her life the last time.

She glanced back down at the card.

This isn't about seduction, Charlie.

She thrust out her jaw. *Good.*

It's about you letting your hair down just once and letting someone spoil you. You deserve to be spoiled. You've helped me and Bea so much.

Her stomach softened. Oh! But… 'That's my job.' Even she had to acknowledge, though, that it had gone above and beyond that now. She and Tom had become friends. Firm friends.

If it makes you more comfortable, frame tonight as a thank-you for all the help you've given me.

She pressed a hand to her heart.

I hope to see you at seven.

Tapping the card to her chin, she turned to glance at the box on the table. It was only dinner…

It wasn't Tom who came to collect her at seven but a member of the hotel staff, who escorted her to the hotel's most exclusive restaurant on the second floor. She was led across the tastefully extravagant room to a private nook beside a floor-to-ceiling window. Cast-iron screens artistically swathed with greenery and fairy lights separated them from the other diners. Behind it stood a single table draped with a crisp white cloth, the dinnerware gleaming in the candlelight. 'Oh! It's so pretty.'

Tom rose from the table. He wore dark trousers in the finest wool and a button-down shirt in the same dusky pink as her dress that highlighted his tan and picked out the grey in his eyes. Those eyes roved over her now and her mouth went dry.

He took in the deep vee of her neckline, the dress's tiny shell buttons and the gentle shirring at its sides, the way it nipped in at the waist and then fell to float about her calves, and nodded. 'You look beautiful, Charlie.'

If she could make her tongue work she'd tell him the dress made her feel like a princess, but his gaze now rested on her mouth. Hunger flared in his eyes as if he'd like to kiss the soft pink lipstick from her lips. Need and heat welled inside her. She wanted him to kiss her. She wanted him to claim her lips with his and make love to her in this private nook and—

'You're stunning, Charlie.'

Reining in her rampant desires, she dragged in a much-needed breath. 'It's the dress.'

'It's not the dress. It's you. The dress is lovely, but you're beautiful.'

Her cheeks heated and her tongue became huge and useless. 'I—' She had to clear her throat and swallow.

As if to give her a moment to compose herself, he held out her chair. She sat, and he moved back to his own seat.

'Thank you, Tom. For the compliment, for the dress, and for tonight. It's all totally unnecessary, but…lovely.'

'Ah, but its loveliness is due in large part to its lack of necessity.'

He poured them both a glass of champagne and raised his glass. 'To enjoying unnecessary indulgences.'

She touched her glass to his.

'Hungry?'

His eyes danced and she wasn't sure why. 'Famished.'

His mouth hooked up into an intriguingly wide grin. 'Excellent.'

Why was he grinning like that? What had he—?

Her starter was placed in front of her and she blinked. Resting on her plate were three of the largest king prawns she'd ever seen. Her mind flashed back to that seemingly innocuous conversation of the previous evening and her jaw dropped. 'You haven't!'

He raised his hands in mock surrender. 'Guilty as charged.'

The warmth of his grin turned her inside out. 'When did you organise all of this?'

'I concocted the plan as soon as you ordered that ridiculous salad last night.'

'There was nothing ridiculous about it.' She pointed at him. 'This trip was already costing you enough and as I was responsible for—'

'*We're* responsible for it, Charlie. *We* have a vested interest in whatever it is Fraser has been doing, not just you.'

He was right.

'But there's nothing wrong with enjoying ourselves along the way. So stop your bellyaching and eat your prawns. Want to try a mussel?'

'I'm not bellyaching. And yes, please.'

The mussel was so delicious they shared their entrées.

When her plate of Sydney rock oysters arrived, though, she pretended to shield them from him. 'I'm not sharing these. You'll have to pry one from my cold dead fingers first.'

'Not even one? Not even if I asked really nicely?'

'Maybe if you asked *really* nicely…'

'Dear angel fairy princess Charlie, who leaves rainbows, butterflies and bluebirds in her wake—'

'Enough!' Charlie laughed and pushed the plate towards him. 'Have two.'

He grinned again and she really wished he'd stop it. Those smiles made her feel as if she was at the centre of the world. She couldn't let herself fall under that spell and believe it. She *wasn't* at the centre of Tom's world. He was just being nice.

'Just teasing—they're all yours.'

They were both quiet as they ate. Charlie relished every glorious mouthful. There was crusty artisan bread as well and a delicious salad that included such exotic morsels as pomegranate seeds and toasted pine nuts. She had a feeling she'd remember this meal for the rest of her life.

When her desert arrived—sticky toffee pudding—she blew out a breath. 'I'm full to bursting, but I can't let this go to waste.'

She sampled it and groaned out loud. *So* good. Glancing across, she found Tom staring at her, an odd expression on his face. He straightened and gestured. 'Tuck in.'

She set her spoon down instead, fighting a frown. 'Why did you do all of this?' He'd gone to so much trouble.

For two heartbeats, his eyes throbbed into hers. 'For all of the reasons previously stated.' He twirled his spoon in his fingers. 'Because I could. And because it's nice to see you enjoying yourself.' His expression grew serious. 'And maybe because you don't ever ask for much, Charlie.' She wanted to fidget under that gaze. 'You should ask for more.'

'I don't need more. I have everything I need.' Or she would have once she'd pulled Melaleuca from the brink of disaster.

'Or you could be afraid you won't get whatever it is you ask for.'

His words left a tiny sting in their wake. Ever since Connor, she'd kept her expectations…low. She picked up her spoon again. 'Or,' she countered, 'you could be so used to people asking you for things, expecting things from you, and expecting you to pick up the tab, that you don't know how to deal with it when nothing is demanded of you.'

He eased back and then huffed out a laugh. 'Touché, but…have you enjoyed tonight?'

'Very much.' She hesitated. 'It's been magical. Thank you, Tom.'

He waved that away. 'You've already thanked me.'

'Ah, but earlier was me just being polite. This is me now being sincere. This whole day has been glorious.'

Something in his face softened. 'You're welcome, Charlie. It's nice to prove the city has its advantages too.'

She chewed over his words. He clearly loved city life, but he'd enjoyed being back at Kings Reach as well. His life might now be in the city, but some instinct told her he needed to protect and nurture what he felt for Kings Reach. She rested her elbows on the table. 'Will you let me return the favour and plan an outing for when we're back at Kings Reach?'

He blinked. 'I—'

'It'll be fun. And after all of this,' she gestured around, 'it'd be churlish to refuse.'

He sent her another one of those pulse-fizzing grins. 'Well, I wouldn't want to be churlish.'

Tom's gaze settled on Charlie as the truck rattled along the gravel road. It was the first Saturday after their return from Melbourne and Fitz had jumped at the chance to spend another day with Bea. Charlie didn't take the turn that led to Fitz's eco-accommodation and his lips pursed.

Not taking her eyes off the road, Charlie raised an eyebrow. 'What?'

'You do know I'm familiar with Kings Reach land, right?'

'Of course you are. But how long has it been since you visited Mitchell's Corner or Emu Springs?'

He scratched his head. 'I…'

She pulled the truck to a halt ninety minutes later and Tom helped unload the horses and saddle them. Mitchell's Corner and Emu Springs, huh? Both places bordered their individual properties. Were they special to her? Had she ever taken her city boy there?

He fought a scowl.

'Who do you wanna ride?'

'Lady, if that's okay.' He enjoyed her sass.

Once mounted, she turned them towards a spot on the river that was easy to ford. Red gums with their enormous girths and generous canopies rose up all around them. The raucous cry of a corella interrupted the bell-like calls of the rosellas. In the city, he didn't hear the birds. He hadn't realised how much he missed that.

He glanced across at Charlie, and lost the battle he'd been having with himself. 'Tell me about the jerk who broke your heart.'

Hooded eyes met his. 'Why?'

'Curiosity, I suppose. It's fine if you don't want to talk about it, but...'

His words trailed off and she rolled her shoulders. 'I'll tell you about Connor if you tell me about Madeline.'

He swallowed. People rarely asked him about Madeline. Her name usually had his insides screwing up tight. But not today. And he had no idea why not.

In the distance a flock of emus paced in loose, unhurried formations while a lone eagle soared high above. He didn't know why he felt so damn relaxed, but what the heck? He'd just roll with it. 'I met Madeline at a low point in my life—just after Mum died. Mum's death hit me hard.'

'I'm sorry about your mum, Tom. Her passing hit the whole district hard. She was a lovely woman.'

'You knew her?'

The swift smile on her lips tugged at him in funny ways. 'I met her a few times. She presented me with the ribbons for the campdrafting and barrel-racing events that I won at Kununurra Show over the years. She always remembered my name. It's just a little thing, but it always made me…'

'What?'

'You're going to think it silly, but it made me feel important—memorable somehow. It was a nice thing to do. And because of her, I try to remember people's names now as well.'

He shook his head. 'Not silly.' To realise that elements of his mother lived on in people like Charlie, to hear proof of the influence she'd had, made him proud.

They'd reached the base of the ridge. Sheer red cliffs towered above them, but Charlie led them to a track that would take them over a low shoulder of the ridge. 'It must've been hard to lose her. I'm glad you found some comfort in Madeline.'

That's right, they were talking about Madeline. He pulled in a breath. 'First thing that struck me about Madeline was her beauty.'

'I saw your wedding photos in the papers—they were everywhere out here; the main source of conversation for at least a month.'

Of course they were.

'The two of you made a striking couple—like a fairy-tale prince and princess. And as I was imagining my own matrimonial dreams at the time, I took a particularly keen interest.'

If he wanted to know what had happened to her matrimonial dreams, he needed to keep talking. 'Madeline made me laugh. She had this knack for saying exactly the right thing at the right time and diffusing the tension. When we were kids, I was the joker—always trying to get a laugh. After Mum died it was as if I'd forgotten how to laugh. Madeline took on the role of joker for me.'

'That sounds nice.'

'It was for a while.'

She turned in the saddle to survey him, sucked her bottom lip into her mouth, worried at it with her teeth. All the things he'd like to do with that mouth—and the rest of Charlie—swamped him. He forced his gaze back to the landscape, did what he could to keep his voice even. 'I mistook Madeline's ability to make me laugh, along with our physical compatibility, to mean we had a deeper connection than we actually did. The truth was she had a list of requirements she wanted in a husband, and I ticked all of the boxes. Number one on that list was having a lot of money and being able to give her the lifestyle she wanted.'

'Ouch.'

Ouch indeed.

'But, Tom, I bet one of those things was to actually *like* the man she married.'

'You'd have thought so, but I'm guessing that didn't make it to number two on her list, because once we were married she set about turning me into her version of an ideal husband.' He hadn't been good enough for Madeline in the same way he hadn't been good enough for his father. He'd thought he'd left his old childhood feelings of inadequacy behind, but during his marriage they'd all come rushing back to the fore.

A frown made deep indents on her brow. 'Which was?'

He bit back a smile at her appalled fascination. 'Someone who loved parties and balls, lavish dinners—who liked being seen in all of the right places—who'd whisk her off on exotic holidays at a moment's notice.'

'And that's not you?'

'I'm more of a quiet-night-in kind of guy.' He shrugged. 'And, while I wouldn't call myself a workaholic, the success of my company means a lot to me. And that means I sometimes put in long hours.'

Charlie nodded as if his priorities made perfect sense.

'I discovered too late that we didn't have anything of substance in common. I discovered too late that I didn't really like her.'

'Oh, Tom.'

Her quiet sympathy soothed the ache at the centre of him. 'I considered divorce, but then she told me she was pregnant with Bea. So I hunkered down and made the best of it instead.'

'But it wasn't the dream.'

'Didn't mean it was a nightmare either.' He rubbed the back of his neck. 'And it might not make sense, but I was gutted when she died— gutted that Bea had lost her mother.' In the distance he could hear the sound of running water and he focused on that for a moment before continuing. 'She was only thirty-two. It felt like such a waste. All because of a stupid accident. She'd bought these new shoes—ridiculously high stilettos. She was so chuffed with them.' Acid burned his stomach. 'The heel twisted in a rug, she lost her balance and fell, hitting her head on a marble coffee table. Here one moment and gone the next.'

Charlie reined Frank to a halt. Reaching across, she pulled Lady to a halt too, and then squeezed his hand. 'I never thought you'd be anything but devastated, Tom.'

'I wasn't as devastated as I would've been if I'd been madly in love with her, though.' He turned his hand, trapping hers inside it. 'I've made her sound cold and calculating, but…she was just seeking the things she thought would make her happy—like the rest of us. I'd been searching for something to fill the hole left after Mum's death, and that wasn't fair to her. I was just as much to blame for our marriage not being the roaring success we'd hoped it'd be.'

'The two of you made the same mistake thousands of people have made. Learn from your mistakes instead of beating yourself up. And don't get Madeline's accident mixed up with your marital difficulties. Those two things aren't related. Madeline didn't trip and fall because the two of you weren't as compatible as you'd once thought. She tripped and fell because she was wearing silly shoes. It should never have ended so tragically. The fact it did isn't anyone's fault.'

Lady stamped a foot and he realised he still had hold of Charlie's hand. He released it, hoping he hadn't squeezed the life out of it. Logically he knew he wasn't to blame for Madeline's accident. He also knew he suffered from a form of survivor's guilt, which made no sense, but grief and guilt could become oddly skewed.

Learn from your mistakes…

'It's why I've no intention of ever remarrying.'

She made a strangled sound. 'Overreaction much?'

'Maybe.' But if he didn't marry, he wouldn't find himself in a bad marriage. 'But it's not just my own happiness I'm responsible for now.'

'Bea,' she murmured.

His father might've considered him a failure as a son. Madeline might've considered him a failure as a husband. But he'd never give Bea cause to think he'd failed her as a father. 'My remarrying would have a major impact on her life.'

'Yeah, but that impact can be positive. To have someone love her as much as you do, to share the load, and the possibility of giving Bea siblings… Not to mention showing her what a loving partnership looks like. Those are big things, Tom.'

'But if I got it wrong…' Ice traced a path down his spine. 'I'm aware of my blessings. I'll settle for what I do have.'

Rounding a wide bend, they emerged into a

clearing. Directly ahead of them a wall of water cascaded from a ledge twenty feet above. Emu Springs. Tom's breath caught. He hadn't been here in more than fifteen years, and for the life of him he couldn't remember why not. All around them palm trees soared and ferns ran riot. He dismounted in a trance.

Charlie dismounted too, smiled at whatever she saw in his face. 'Hungry?'

'Famished.' Echoing her words in Melbourne. He was hungry with an urgent need to reconnect with all the places of his youth.

Before they were lost to him forever?

'I know it's not a smart restaurant or an art gallery—'

He pressed a hand to her mouth. 'It's perfect.'

Her breath tickled his fingers and her eyes went wide. She raised her hands in surrender. Dropping his own hand, he backed up a step. They spun away and both busied themselves with *things*. He strode across to the rock pool and Charlie unloaded the saddlebags with their lunch.

He didn't return until he had the thumping of his heart under control. Charlie had started a campfire and set a billy to boil for tea. Settling on a rock, he gestured to the waterfall. 'It's amazing to be here again.'

Her lips twitched. 'I'm not going to say I told you so.' And then she gestured to the food she'd laid out—cold chicken, potato salad, tomatoes and cucumber, homemade bread. 'It's not fancy, but it should be good.'

His mouth watered. 'It's a bit fancy by Kimberley standards. You wouldn't eat like this on muster.'

'This is a picnic, not work.' She winked. 'And it's a bit fancy as I cooked the chicken, baked the bread and made the potato salad myself.'

She had?

'Because I'm a woman of action…'

'Not a cowpat,' he finished on a laugh.

He attacked the food with gusto. Every damn thing tasted like the best thing he'd ever eaten. When she asked if he wanted cake or fruit, he shook his head and patted his stomach. '*So* full.'

She made the tea—strong and hot—and handed him a mug before stretching out on the ground, her back to a rock. He wouldn't mind a nap, except… 'Your turn,' he said.

She blew on her tea. 'You're referring to my city boy?'

He nodded.

'There's not really much to tell.'

He didn't believe that for a moment. 'You were fifteen when you met?'

'We were both at school in Kununurra—boarded with different families through the week and went home for the weekends. His father had bought the station on our north-east boundary. Connor and I… Well… We just clicked. From the moment we met neither of us had eyes for anyone else. He'd originally been from Brisbane, but took to country life as if he'd been born to it and...'

Her lips twisted and he fought a scowl. 'And?'

'When we finished high school we did business courses by correspondence and threw ourselves into working on our respective stations until we had enough money to buy a truck. We hit the road as stockman and stockwoman for hire—travelled all over the Kimberley. It was brilliant.'

He imagined the freedom of it and the youthful optimism—the sleeping under the stars, the impromptu swims in waterholes, the sights they'd have seen. 'How long did you do that for?'

'Four years. Until we were twenty-five. The plan was to save madly and buy a place of our own. Then we'd get married, have a couple of kids, live happily ever after.'

An ache started up at the centre of him. 'What happened?'

She watched the red-backed fairy wrens dancing in the undergrowth. 'While we were away his father sold up and moved back to Brisbane. Wanted to be closer to his ageing parents. Connor went to visit him.'

She remained quiet for so long the ache in his chest became a burn. 'Something happen on that visit?' Had he *cheated* on her?

'He never came back.'

He blinked...straightened. 'He what?'

'He rang to say he was sorry, but that he wanted a different life now. He told me to keep the truck and his horse—and then he took half our money along with an over-inflated guestimate of what said truck and horse were worth.'

Tom carefully set his tea on the ground before he could spill it. 'He broke up with you, after ten years together, *over the phone*?'

'Classy, huh?'

'That's the lowest of the low.' His mind reeled. What an awful thing to do.

She sipped her tea. 'You know what really stung? He never asked me to join him. Obviously *I* wasn't part of the new life he wanted.'

He couldn't imagine Charlie anywhere but here. She belonged to the Kimberley in the same way the red gums and the gorge country did. He rubbed a hand through his hair. 'Would you have gone if he had?'

'No idea. But the fact he didn't ask me made me realise he'd never loved me the way I'd loved him. There must've always been a part of him he'd hidden away from me. Whereas I…' Her laugh made him wince. 'I held nothing back.'

The jerk had made her feel like a fool. 'You're worth ten of him, Charlie.'

'Absolutely.' But she said it more for form's sake.

'You ought to be proud of yourself.' Wrapping his hands around his hot mug, he welcomed the burn against his palms. 'You had to start from scratch. You had to create a whole new plan for your life, and you've done it with grit and class.'

Her chin came up. 'It's why I have to keep reminding myself that you're a city boy, Tom.'

'No, I'm not. I'm a country boy who just happens to live in the city.'

She sent him a sidelong glance. 'Frame it however you like. You live in the city—that makes you a city boy.'

He wanted to rage against her assessment.

'Even if you were sticking around, it doesn't change the fact that there's no room in your life for someone like me.'

He went cold all over. He'd lost too many people that he'd loved. He didn't think he had the resources to lose another or to feel as if he'd hadn't lived up to their expectations. Regardless of where he lived, there was no room for Charlie in his life. Squaring his shoulders, he nodded. 'You're right.'

CHAPTER TEN

After packing up their lunch, Charlie and Tom set off for their next stop. She kept flicking glances at Tom whenever she thought he wasn't looking. He kept flicking glances at her. *It had to stop.*

They reined in when they reached Mitchell's Corner, both exhaling at the same time. Strange rock formations sprang out of the red earth like giant termite nests and growing among them were boab trees with their massive bottle-shaped trunks. 'It's really something, isn't it?' she murmured.

'Awe-inspiring is what springs to mind.' His voice was as hushed as hers.

They remained silent for a long time, just taking it in, and then Charlie reached out and touched his arm, pointing to the boulders off to their left.

'A rock wallaby.' Everything about him sharpened. 'Now, that's something you don't see every day.'

Sightings were rare, and it felt like a benediction. So did Tom's fierce gaze as he took it all in—gobbling it up like a starving man.

She thought of all he must be going through and an ache stretched through her. 'I'm sorry, Tom. To be in danger of losing all of this…' He might now live in the city, but this was his family home—it's where he'd been born, where he'd grown up. It had to feel like a part of him.

He rubbed a hand over his face. 'I've never been forced to confront how I'd feel if we lost Kings Reach.' Weariness etched itself into the lines fanning out from his eyes and mouth, and her ache grew jagged edges. 'I'm shocked at how much the place still means to me. I *don't* want to lose it.'

'It might never come to that. Logan says the trust can't be broken. And even if it can, do you really think Jack would do something drastic when he knows how much the station means to the rest of you?'

She might not know Jack, but she knew Tom and Fitz. If Jack was even a tenth of the men they were he'd never do such a thing.

Tom's hands clenched about the reins, though he was careful to keep the bit loose in Lady's mouth. 'I can't predict what Jack will do, haven't the faintest idea where his head is at. I don't know if he'd agree to sell his share to the rest of us. Or…'

He turned grey and she wanted to hug him.

'He fell out with Dad so badly. And before the ball, he hadn't been back in over twenty years.

Even now he continues to hold himself aloof from the rest of us. I just...'

Her eyes stung at the unspoken pain in his words.

'For all I know he'd love to see the place go to rack and ruin, or diced up and sold off piecemeal. Hell, maybe he truly does want to burn it to the ground.'

To lose Melaleuca due to a series of unforeseen disasters would be awful. But to lose it because of a brother's anger and rage? Pulling in a breath, she squared her shoulders. 'Jack is a lot of things, but he's not an idiot. And he *did* come home for your mother's ball. That proves he still has some sense of connection to the place *and* to all of you. He might not show it, but he still cares—even if he doesn't want to. And whatever else he thinks, Jack's not going to be able to avoid his brothers forever.'

He glanced across.

'Three Kings against one? The man doesn't stand a chance.' Her words had him huffing out a laugh. 'Come on, we've one more stop to make and it's the perfect spot for afternoon tea.'

Twenty minutes later, Charlie pulled them to a halt at the bottom of a low rise. 'You ready?'

His lips twitched. 'I do know what's on the other side.'

'Ah, but have you ever seen it from this particular vantage point?' She urged Frank forward, Tom and Lady keeping perfect pace beside them, and they crested the rise together. Dropping the reins, she spread her hands. 'Emu Springs, Mitchell's Corner…and now *this*.'

A vast wetland spread before them all the way to a hazy spot in the distance. In the early morning the mist would rise and hover above it—turning the air hazy and golden—but she loved what it looked like now when the air was clear and every colour crisp and distinct. 'It blows me away every single time I see it.'

The wetlands of the Kimberley were vast wild places, and they teemed with life. Tom studied it all as if committing the colours, the sounds, the sight, to memory. She could see in his face how much he missed all of this. The bombshell Fraser had dropped in his sons' laps could detonate at any moment. She didn't want Tom hurt in the ensuing explosion.

Her heart clenched. He'd been hurt enough—his fractured family, his disaster of a marriage, his relentless efforts to be the perfect father. That was enough for anyone to deal with. To now face the possibility of losing his home…

He glanced across. 'You don't have anything like this on Melaleuca?'

'These are the closest wetlands to Melaleuca.' Birds fluttered in and out of the rushes and reeds below. Stilts made their funny long-legged progress through the shallows, the blue of a kingfisher's wings flashed in the sun. She shot him a wry grin. 'And as our boundary is just over there, I can sneak across for a look whenever the mood takes me.'

Her words made his eyes dance. 'You have my unreserved permission to wander at will on Kings Reach land. For as long as it's my permission to give.'

Oh, lord, this man could make her melt. 'Thanks, Tom.' She lifted her nose in the air. 'We might not have wetlands, but I'll have you know that Melaleuca does have some of the grandest river country you'll ever see. Grander even than Kings Reach.'

He feigned shock. 'Surely not. I'll have you know that Kings Reach is God's own country.'

She couldn't help but laugh. 'You grew up with that too, huh?'

'Heard it at least once a week.'

'We have some waterholes that would make you pea green.' Even though that was true, and although Melaleuca Downs also had excellent grazing land, Fraser had more than enough of both on Kings Reach. He had more than he was currently using. She couldn't see any conceivable reason why he'd want to add Melaleuca Downs to his portfolio or why he'd want to make things difficult for his neighbours.

And she and Tom needed to get to the bottom of that. 'If you don't believe me, come over and see for yourself some time.'

He turned in the saddle. 'You mean that?'

'Absolutely.' Did he doubt it? 'You'd be welcome any time.'

He stared at her as if it was a big deal and she had to fight the urge to fidget. It *wasn't* a big deal. It was just…hospitality.

'Come on, there's the prettiest clearing further along.'

When they reached it she led him to the perfect spot—thickly grassed with a glorious view. Below them, two black swans glided on the water. The air was filled with warbling, cheeping and whistling, punctuated here and there with a guttural squawk of a heron or the strange cry of a curlew. The horses grazed nearby. Unwrapping the package she'd pulled from her saddlebag that contained thick slices of the cake she'd made, she held it out to him. 'I give you…lemon drizzle cake!'

His slow grin had her pulse dancing. He reached for a slice, raised it to his lips, took a bite, and chewed. He held her gaze the entire time and she held her breath until the moment he closed his eyes and moaned. 'God, Charlie, this is the best cake *ever*.'

The breath left her on a whoosh and her pulse pitter-pattered like a mad thing. Seizing a slice of her own, she took a big bite in the hope it would hide her delight in the compliment.

'You haven't been able to find the secret compartment, then?'

'Nothing. Nada. Zilch. Utterly infuriating. Are you sure there's another one?'

His chuckle brushed over her like a promise. 'I'll show you where it is when we get back.'

She tried to keep her voice casual. 'Did you check it? It doesn't hide a key to Fraser's office?'

He shook his head, took another slice of cake. 'Just another toy soldier.'

She should let him enjoy the peace and quiet, the serenity of being in this beautiful place. But time was running out. For both of them. She took a long drink from her water bottle, before recapping it. 'What do you propose we do now? We've not been able to find evidence that Fraser has reneged on any other contracts. Nobody's talking.' Fraser, it seemed, was untouchable.

'Ah, I've been thinking about that.'

Tom stretched out, the picture of indolent idleness, and a startling surge of adrenaline had her pulse quickening and fingers curling into her palms. She had to swallow before she could speak. 'And?'

He raised an eyebrow.

'Have you come up with a plan?'

He grinned. 'Of course I have. Charlie, it's time for direct action.'

Tom moved up behind Charlie, doing his best not to inhale her scent too deeply, while Bea spun in a circle nearby. 'Ready?' he murmured.

Glancing around, she nodded, before clapping her hands. 'Let's play hopscotch, Bea!'

Bea stopped spinning to bounce. 'Yes!'

The moment Annalise came down the front steps, Tom intercepted her. 'Hey, Annalise, you ever play hopscotch?'

She shook her curtain of blonde hair over her shoulder, but her lips twitched when she saw the game Bea and Charlie were playing. 'A long time ago, Tom.'

'Were you any good?' Annalise looked fit, as if she'd rock a yoga or pump class. Or both, one after the other.

'I could hold my own.'

'Then be a sport and come give Charlie a run for her money.'

'I'm supposed to be working—'

'It'll take…what—fifteen or twenty minutes? Charlie's bragging she's the hopscotch champion of the Kimberley and Bea is now desperate to beat her.'

Annalise laughed. 'Charlie's a smart cookie.'

Of course she was. She was brilliant!

'Getting Bea to practise skills like that…' Her hands went to her hips. 'She'd have made a great schoolteacher.'

The thought of Charlie cooped up in a schoolroom somewhere made him frown. She needed to be free to come and go beneath a blue sky whenever she wanted.

'She'll make a great mum.'

Now, that he *could* see—Charlie surrounded by a brood of laughing, curly-haired kids with sunshine in their smiles and mischief in their eyes, following her as if she were the Pied Piper. He wouldn't mind following her—

Don't go there. 'The thing is, I want someone to show Bea that one day she can be every bit as good.'

'Tom, I'm working and—'

'But of course, if you're busy...' He infused his shrug with disappointment. 'Or afraid of being shown up.'

That pointed chin lifted. 'I'm not afraid.'

Something inside him shifted. 'My father hasn't shown much interest in getting to know his granddaughter. Has he asked you to stay away from her too?'

A martial light came into her eyes. 'You are wrong about *so* many things.'

'Like what?'

She didn't give him an answer, not that he expected one. But she did slap the folders she carried to his chest. 'Hold these!' Before striding towards Bea and Charlie. 'Move over, lovely ladies—I used to be a dab hand at hopscotch.'

Bea and Charlie cheered. Tom let out a breath. *Mission accomplished.*

He waited until the game had started, before slipping inside and trying the handle to his father's office. The door swung open. Depositing the folders on the desk, he immediately made for the filing cabinets and opened the first drawer.

'What the hell are you looking for?'

Fraser. Closing his eyes, he bit back a curse before turning. 'I heard you'd agreed to lease Sid Ashwell a parcel of land. And that you reneged on the deal after he'd brought in new stock.' Leaning back against the cabinet, he folded his arms. 'I wanted to see the proof with my own eyes. Why would you do one of our neighbours such a bad turn?'

Fraser's shoulders sagged and it was as if he aged before Tom's eyes. '*This* is the kind of man you think me?'

His heart pounded in bruising thumps against his ribs. 'How would I know? I barely know you any more.'

Fraser moved behind his desk, lowered himself to his chair. 'It's under M for Melaleuca Downs.'

Tom retrieved the file. 'What am I supposed to think?' He swung back to his father. 'You clearly don't want me here. You've avoided my every attempt to talk to you. You don't make an effort with Bea. And that's before we get to the issue of the irrevocable trust.' He found himself breathing hard. Moving across to the desk, he planted himself in the seat opposite. 'Why wouldn't I think the worst of you?'

Fraser opened his mouth, closed it; rubbed a hand over his face. 'Hell, Tom, it's not that I don't want you here. It's just... I look at you and I see your mother. That's not your fault, but I miss her every single day, and sometimes when I catch sight of you my heart leaps. And then I remember she's no longer with us and…'

Tom swallowed. Fraser looked lost in a way he'd never seen before.

'It's not personal. It's not you, it's me.'

'I thought you blamed me.'

'*Blamed* you?'

'For her death. At the funeral you said I should've been here. You said that if I'd been here, I'd have seen she was sicker than she'd let on.'

'No, son. *No!* God, Tom. That was me lashing out and railing at the world and you just happened to be in the firing line. I apologised afterwards. I thought by now you'd understand.' His hands clenched. 'You've lost a wife too. I wish you'd been spared that.'

And yet he hadn't loved Madeline the way Fraser had loved Eliza.

Fraser huffed out a mirthless laugh. 'I was always envious of you, you know? You could make your mother laugh when I could barely make her smile. You two were close and I felt…left out.'

He stared at his father in disbelief.

'It made your mother happy to know you were out in the world living your life. It's what she wanted for you. You were her strength and her support after Will died. I know you felt it your job to make up for my deficiencies—so your brothers had someone to turn to—and that meant you stayed on longer than you should've.'

Had the world stopped turning?

'She was so proud of how successful you were. She wanted to hide how ill she was from all of us.'

His chest burned. He had no idea what to say.

'I know you all blamed me for Will's death,' Fraser said.

Tom dragged in a steadying breath. He *could* talk about this. 'I know you didn't mean for the accident to happen. We all do.'

'Doesn't change the fact that a single act of temper on my part led to Will's accident.'

'Since having Bea, I know now how crazy kids can make you. But, Dad, our problems—mine and yours—started before Will's death.'

Fraser straightened, some of his colour returning. 'What are you talking about?'

'A couple of months before Will's accident, I overheard you tell Mum you'd have to find a job for me away from the station.'

Fraser's jaw dropped.

'I'd fallen off my horse—'

'Counting galahs, as I remember.'

He remembered? 'This was my home!' He slapped a hand to his chest. 'And you didn't want me here.'

Fraser shot to his feet. 'That's not what I meant!' His eyes flashed. 'Damn it, Tom, why the hell didn't you talk to me about it?'

'Oh, like you're a model of communication!'

Fraser thumped down into his chair again. 'Oh, Tom—' grief stretched his voice thin '—I remember that day so clearly, because it was the day I realised how smart you were. It was the day I realised working the station would never fulfil you. You probably had the best seat on a horse out of any of your brothers, you never shirked hard work—always rose to the challenge—but station work never captured you the way it did Jack.'

He stared at his father and wondered if he'd ever really known him. 'But the tone of your voice…' It had been so bitter. It had left him feeling less—as if he'd failed somehow.

'I expect I was trying to cover up my disappointment. Men of my generation weren't supposed to show emotion.' His eyes sharpened. 'And before you misinterpret that, I wasn't disappointed in *you*. I was proud of you. But the knowledge you wouldn't always be here working alongside me… I don't doubt that my voice would've sounded harsh and bitter to your ears. I'm sorry, Tom.'

Tom stared and the world shifted on its axis. He swore loudly. 'For all of these years I thought whenever you looked at me what you saw was a failure.'

Fraser's chin lifted. 'What I saw was a self-made man with a business acumen that left me speechless!'

What a damn waste.

'As for not making an effort with Bea—' Fraser

thrust his jaw out '—I figured you wouldn't want me anywhere near your daughter. I figured you wouldn't trust me after what happened with Will.'

'You thought wrong.' As the words left him, he realised he meant them.

A cautious hope lit Fraser's eyes. 'So I can talk to her, tell her stories…play games with her?'

'It'll make her day. She's been asking me and Charlie why you don't like her.'

Fraser's jaw sagged. He snapped it back into place. 'We can't have her thinking that! I'll rectify it immediately.'

'Good.'

The eyes on the other side of the table turned contemplative. 'Speaking of Charlie, I get the impression she means a lot to you.'

Things inside him scrunched up tight. 'She's become a good friend.' *She's more than that.* He shook that off. 'One can never have too many friends.'

Fraser started and swore softly. 'That—' he pinched his nose between thumb and forefinger '—is true.'

Tom's gaze dropped to the file. 'So what's this about?' He held it up.

With what seemed like an effort, Fraser lifted his head. 'You still think I'd break my word?'

'You promised Mum you'd organise the irrevocable trust. You promised that each of her sons would have an equal share and say in the station's future. You're going back on your word to her now.'

Dark eyes turned flinty. 'I promised your mother a lot of things.'

'If you broke your word to her, then breaking your word to Sid Ashwell isn't a huge leap.'

Fraser gestured at the file. 'You'd better read it, then.'

Pulling out the enclosed documents, Tom read over them. A chill chased down his spine. 'This…'

Fraser's nostrils flared. 'I'll leave you to decide what to do—'

'Wait, Annalise! We—'

Annalise burst into the room to glare at Tom, 'You tricked me!'

'Guilty as charged.'

Behind Annalise, Charlie mouthed *Sorry*.

It was all Tom could do not to drop his head to the desk and close his eyes.

CHAPTER ELEVEN

The expression on Tom's face had Charlie's chest clenching. Whatever he'd discovered, whatever words he and his father had just exchanged, they'd hurt him. She should never have dragged him into her sordid little search.

Not sordid. It wasn't wrong to seek justice. Pop had worked hard his entire life; he'd done right by everyone his entire life. He deserved the same in return. Besides, Tom was seeking justice of his own. She glanced at the file he held and swallowed. Was that...?

Annalise turned her glare on Charlie. 'And you were in on it.'

'You know what, Annalise,' she stuck out a hip, 'you're a bit rusty, but if you put in some practice you could be a hopscotch contender.'

Annalise rolled her eyes, but not before Charlie glimpsed a smile there.

Bea came barrelling into the room to glare at all of them. 'Why did you run away? We haven't finished our game.'

Charlie might want to snatch that file out of

Tom's hands and devour it in one fell swoop, but she had a job to do. 'Sorry, Honey Bea, we remembered something we had to sort out. I think Annalise has to get back to work now, though.'

Annalise nodded.

'So we'll have to challenge her to a game when she's free. It's just you and me, kiddo.'

Tom stared at her as if her upbeat manner was the eighth wonder of the world. Considering what he held, she almost agreed with him. But Bea didn't deserve to have her equilibrium disturbed by the complicated relationships in the room. She deserved rainbows and unicorns and pony rides and puppies. And hopscotch.

She sent Tom a buck-up smile. It didn't seem to help, though, and her heart burned. Regardless of how he felt about his father, discovering Fraser's dishonesty had to be a blow.

'Before we head back to our game, maybe we can ask Grandad if he has a free window tomorrow for another game of Go Fish?'

Bea swung to her grandfather. 'Can you?'

'*Please,*' Tom groaned. 'Remember your manners, Bea.'

'*Please*, Grandad.'

'Well, let's see…' Fraser pulled his diary towards him and pretended to consult it. 'I can be at your disposal any time in the afternoon, so if there's a particular time that suits, let me know. I'll look forward to it.'

Bea turned a beaming face up to Charlie, waiting for her to answer. 'I…' Fraser's good humour had taken her off guard.

'What about now?' Tom said. 'The three of you—' he motioned at Bea, Fraser and Annalise '—could have morning tea and play Go Fish?'

Charlie blinked.

'Excellent idea!' Fraser shot to his feet and came around the desk, holding out his hand to Bea. 'Will you do me the honour of joining me for tea and cake, Princess Bea?'

Bea glanced up at Charlie, searching for direction. Charlie bent down to whisper in her ear. The little girl straightened. 'I'd be…delighted.' She stumbled over the last word, but beamed up at them all as if proud of herself. Taking her grandfather's hand, she skipped him out of the office.

'Come along, Annalise,' Fraser called over his shoulder, just as the other woman opened her mouth—probably to demand of Tom and Charlie what was going on.

On impulse, Charlie reached across and squeezed her hand. 'Our tricking you wasn't personal, Annalise. Please don't be angry. I'd hate for you to feel hurt.'

Annalise blinked and then squeezed Charlie's hand back before following Bea and Fraser.

Tom moved across to Charlie and she blew out a breath. 'What have you done to the real Fraser?' she murmured. 'Where have you hidden him?'

'We just had the most extraordinary conversation.'

She turned and realised how closely they'd been drawn unconsciously towards one another. They both took a step back at the same time, looking everywhere but at each other. 'You did?'

'But that's a conversation for another day. C'mon.'

Taking her hand, he led her upstairs to their sitting room, releasing her when they reached it. She curled it inside her other hand—though whether to capture the warmth of his touch or rub it away, she didn't know. He didn't speak immediately and her insides twisted. 'It's worse than we thought, isn't it? Oh, Tom, I *am* sorry.'

'It's not that. I…' He looked utterly at a loss. 'Things aren't exactly as I expected and…'

He dragged a hand through his hair, and a cold fingernail traced a path down her spine. She took the proffered file. Planting herself on the sofa, she opened it and read the documents inside.

That cold fingernail became an icy hand that closed about her chest, squeezing and squeezing.

'Charlie?'

Tom's voice came from a long way away. Instructions to put her head down between her knees while a gentle voice counted breaths. Eventually the constriction in her chest eased, allowing her to gulp in a breath that pushed the grey at the edges of her vision away. 'This says—' she straightened '—Pop couldn't afford to pay the lease.'

'I'm sorry, Charlie. I know this must come as a shock. That you must be feeling...'

Leaping to her feet, she flung the file across the room. 'Furious?' she spat, before pacing from sofa to balcony doors, to the other end of the room and back again. 'I want to tear things with my bare hands and rail at you and Fraser and accuse you of concocting these documents to close ranks and prevent me and Pop from taking action.'

Tom paled.

She stabbed a finger at him. 'I want to accuse you of lying and double-dealing...and I wish that was true.'

No, she didn't. She *really* didn't. But it'd be easier than facing the truth. 'I want to accuse you of forging emails.' She stalked across to where the documents had scattered across the floor and rifled through them. She held one up and read sections out. 'But that's all in Pop's voice. It's how *he* talks.'

They weren't forged. They were real. Tom hadn't lied to her. Fraser hadn't broken his word. The fight went out of her and she dropped back to the sofa. 'Pop lied to me.' *He'd lied.*

'I'm sorry, Charlie.'

She stared at the copy of the email she held—an email pleading for more time—and a lump lodged in her throat. 'Do you know how hard it would've been for him to ask Fraser for an extension on the payment?'

His lips thinned. 'I can guess. And I'm not impressed Fraser didn't grant it.'

'He's known to be a hard man. That's not a surprise.'

'It's not neighbourly.'

'But it's not *illegal*.' She swallowed hard, her eyes burning. 'Why would Pop lie to me? If things are more dire than I thought… Does he think me such a weak and paltry bag of bones that I couldn't understand—or help him?' Pop loved her. She *knew* that. But she'd thought he trusted her too.

'What do you want to do?'

She didn't even have to think about it. 'I need to speak to Pop, face-to-face.' She glanced at her watch. 'If I leave within the next hour, I could be at Melaleuca by four o'clock. Can you spare me for the day, Tom? I can be back by morning and—'

'I'll drive you.'

She stared at him.

'I'm not leaving you to deal with this on your own. You and me, we're friends—a team. I want to come with you—as moral support.'

The burn in her throat and eyes eased a little. 'I'd like that,' she whispered.

'Let me see if I can make arrangements for Bea and—'

'She can come with us.'

He glanced across.

'Mum and Nan will go into ecstasies over her.

Why don't I pack her an overnight bag too and we'll leave in an hour?' she said, heading for Bea's bedroom.

As she moved away from him, though, the new and shocking reality that *Pop had lied to her* descended on her again. Her chest ached as if she'd swallowed broken glass. She had no idea what she'd say to her grandfather when she saw him. But—

'Charlie?'

She glanced around and Tom's jaw clenched at whatever he saw in her face. With a soft curse, he moved across, cupped her face in his hands and swooped down to capture her lips in a kiss. Those magic lips moved over hers with a slow and deliberate warmth that had her head swimming, dulling the spiky thorns in her chest. She drank him in, glorying in his taste and scent.

With another soft curse, he eased away, dropped his hands from her face. 'Sorry, I shouldn't have done that. I wanted to make things better for you.' As he spoke, he moved further away. 'Stupid, huh? A kiss isn't going to make you feel better. Okay, you pack bags for you and Bea and I'll sort out a few things, and get Mrs McRae to pack us something to eat on the road.' And then he was gone.

Charlie touched trembling fingers to her lips. 'I don't know,' she whispered. 'It sure as heck didn't make me feel worse.'

Tom, Bea and Charlie drove into the gates at Melaleuca Downs just before four. Charlie's heart surged against her ribs. She still had no idea what she meant to say to Pop.

'This is your home, Charlie!' Bea bounced on the back seat. 'And you love it with your whole heart.'

'I do.' She'd spent a large portion of the trip telling Bea about Melaleuca, aware that Tom marked her every word.

'I do too,' Bea said, and her automatic loyalty made Charlie smile.

Tom touched her arm and pointed. She followed his finger to find the Kings Reach helicopter sitting in the nearby field. 'Looks like you have company.'

Her stomach clenched. In her search for justice, had she caused trouble for Melaleuca? Had Fraser come to threaten her family or to wreak retribution? Oh, God!

Breathe, Charlie, breathe.

Leading the way into the house in a kind of fog, she braced for the worst. The mood in the living room, though, was far from grim. In fact… She halted. It felt as if they'd walked into the middle of a party!

'Right on time.' Her mother kissed her cheek before bending down. 'And you must be Bea.'

Bea beamed back. 'You're Charlie's mum!'

Vicky Ashwell grinned. 'Spot on! Charlie told me you were smart.'

Bea's chest puffed out. 'Did you teach her to play hopscotch?'

'I did.'

'While I taught her to make lemon drizzle cake,' Nan said, joining them. 'I'm Charlie's nanna.'

'Lemon drizzle cake is Charlie's favourite.' Bea clearly hoped this meant cake would be in the offing.

'Mine is caramel tarts and I started a batch this morning, but I haven't finished putting the caramel into the tart cases. If you'd like to help...'

And just like that Mum and Nan whisked Bea into the kitchen.

Charlie turned to face the men in the room. She still hadn't worked out what to say to Pop, but... Pressing her hands together, she turned to Fraser. 'I owe you an apology. I thought you'd reneged on that deal with Pop. I thought you'd taken him for a ride.'

Fraser nodded. 'You wanted to put things right.'

She'd expected anger, scorn, and some kind of payback. Not understanding.

'That's admirable, Charlie. You know what else is admirable?' He held her gaze. 'You brokered a relationship between me and Bea, even though you didn't like me.'

She rolled her shoulders. 'That's a separate issue. I love my Pop. If Bea could have even a fraction of that with you, then I wanted that for her.'

He pointed a steady finger at her. 'Generous, that's what you are. So's your Pop. So's my son over there. He reminded me of something today. He said one couldn't have too many friends.'

She glanced between Fraser and Pop. Were they now friends? Fraser *wasn't* here to cause trouble?

The weight on her heart lifted. She grinned at Tom, could've hugged him. 'Wise words.'

Nothing about this scene made sense. Tom had walked into the room and Charlie's grandmother had smiled at him and her mother had squeezed his arm and their warmth had wrapped around him, making him feel as if he belonged. Now his father was openly praising him?

'You can't have too many friends.' Fraser shook his head. 'For the last twenty years I've invested in business relationships and political networking, but friends…? Those are thin on the ground.'

It shook Tom to realise he'd been in danger of following in his father's footsteps. He glanced around the Ashwells' unpretentious living room. When Bea brought friends home to visit, he wanted them to feel *this* warmth, *this* welcome.

An image of his stately Victorian terrace in Sydney rose in his mind, and he frowned. The warmth of the Ashwell home was in its openness—it's open-heartedness—which he'd lost somewhere along the way. He wanted to get it back.

'Fact is, I haven't been neighbourly in a decade.' Since Mum had died.

'Though probably longer.'

'Tragedy has touched your life twice, Fraser.' Sid patted the other man's shoulder. 'Your neighbours understand it can be a slow journey out the other side.'

'Fact of the matter is, Charlie, that your Pop once did me a great kindness,' Fraser said. 'But when he asked me for a favour all these years later, I refused. I've sacrificed kindness on the altar of business. While that's made me successful, I'm not well-liked.'

Did that *matter* to his father? Was his father *lonely*?

'My life felt hard and I wanted everyone else's lives to feel hard too. I'm ashamed of myself,' he mumbled, not meeting anyone's gaze.

'What Fraser is trying to say is that he's had a rethink and is now happy to lease Melaleuca that parcel of land on a delayed payment plan,' Sid said.

Tom's shoulders went back. He wanted to clap his father on the shoulder in the same way Sid just had. His father had decided to do the right thing and he was *proud* of him.

Charlie bounced on the balls of her feet for a moment and then leaped forward and kissed Fraser's cheek. 'Thank you. A million times, thank you.'

'Pleasure,' he mumbled, turning red.

Tom didn't think Charlie noticed, though. She'd

spun to her grandfather, raising both hands in a silent question.

'Oh, lass, I'm sorry I lied to you.'

'But...*why* did you lie?'

Tom wanted to wrap her in his arms and wipe away her pain. Charlie didn't deserve pain. She deserved starlit nights and lazy afternoon canters and lemon drizzle cake.

'I didn't want you seeing me as another good-for-nothing man in your life who'd let you down. First your no-good father and then that scoundrel Connor. I felt as if I'd made a right mess of things and I wanted to make them right before you found out. I didn't want you feeling I'd let you down like they had.'

'How could you ever think that? You've stuck beside me my whole life—loved me *my whole life*.'

'I took your money and lost it!'

Her hands went to her hips. 'I invested my money in *my home*. And whatever happened, we'd have fought hard and given it our best shot. But even if we failed, I'd have never blamed you.' Her hands twisted together. 'I thought you didn't trust me. I thought you didn't think I'd be able to help or—'

'Heck, no, Charlie. *Never*.' The older man pulled her into a fierce hug. 'I've been a silly old man wanting to fix everything on my own, too stubborn to ask for help, and not wanting you to see me as anything but indestructible. But you're right, we're in this together, and I lost sight of the fact that you're my greatest strength. Please forgive me.'

Fraser nudged Tom and nodded in the direction of the kitchen. They quietly exited, but not before he heard Charlie say, 'Of course I forgive you.' As if it were the easiest thing in the world to say and do.

He glanced at Fraser. He could forgive him for the events of the past. To know Fraser hadn't wanted him to leave the station, that he'd never considered him lesser or somehow lacking, had lifted a huge weight from his shoulders. But the events of the future still hung between them. Fraser wanted to break the irrevocable trust and, while Tom had every intention of fighting that, he didn't know exactly where that left them now. Except at odds with one another again. It still felt like a mess and yet a new peace had sprung up between them too.

As soon as they entered the kitchen, the Ashwells made room for them at the table. Charlie's mum, Vicky, patted the seat beside her for Fraser, while Charlie's Uncle Wayne indicated Tom should take the chair beside him, immediately engaging him in conversation about the stock market. For once he was happy to give advice away for free. Bea stood at the counter with Charlie's grandmother, filling tart cases with caramel.

Sid and Charlie joined them a short time later, arm-in-arm, and more room was made at the table—and somehow the table didn't become smaller, just more perfect. 'You'll be staying the night, of course,' Vicky said.

Charlie nodded.

'Not me,' Fraser said.

'But you'll stay for dinner,' Charlie's nanna said.

'Right.' Vicky glanced at Tom and Charlie. 'We'll put Bea in your room, Charlie, and you and Tom can bunk down in the old stockman's cottage.'

Charlie blinked, opened her mouth, only to shut it again, a frown in her eyes. She glanced across. 'That okay with you, Tom? I, uh…'

What was wrong?

Her gaze slid away. 'The stockman's cottage is a short walk from the house.'

While Bea would be in the house.

'Bea could come home with me,' Fraser offered.

Bea turned, dripping caramel on the floor. Nobody seemed to mind. 'I want to stay in Charlie's room.'

'Even though your daddy and I won't be in the house?'

He loved that she checked Bea was comfortable with the arrangements. Bea, though, would be in seventh heaven and probably spoiled rotten.

'Auntie Vicky and Nanna can look after me.'

Auntie Vicky and *Nanna?*

'Absolutely,' *Nanna* agreed. 'It's good to have

a littlie in the house again. It's too quiet when the Dudleys are at school.'

That was when it hit him. Why weren't he and Charlie being put up in the Dudleys' bedrooms?

Charlie gave him a quick tour of the cottage—living room, two bedrooms, bathroom, and an eat-in kitchen. She set a bottle of wine to the kitchen bench—the wine her mother had pressed into her hands before literally pushing them out of the door. Even though the night was yet young. *Very* young.

He scrubbed a hand through his hair. 'Are we being set up?'

'Feels a lot like it, doesn't it?' That cute nose wrinkled. 'Probably my fault.'

His stomach became a hard, tense knot. What the hell was that supposed to mean? He and Charlie had set boundaries. They'd both said they didn't want anything more.

When she lifted the wine, he nodded. She poured them both a glass, pushed one towards him. 'Whenever I've rung home recently, I've mentioned you and Bea a lot.' She led the way into the living room. 'Also I'm thirty-one and apparently that means I should be thinking about babies…' She rolled her eyes. 'They'd love to see me settled with some nice man.' Curling up on a seat, she raised her glass in his direction. 'And you're a nice man.'

He lowered himself to the sofa, trying not to frown. *Nice?* He'd prefer hot, irresistible…

She chuckled at whatever she saw in his face. 'It's just wishful thinking on their part, so relax and enjoy a quiet night. I've no plans to seduce you.'

'I wouldn't mind.'

She choked on her wine.

Dammit! What was he thinking? 'Except we rightly agreed that shouldn't happen, so please forget I said that.'

'Already forgotten!'

He fought a frown at the promptness of her reply. Couldn't she look at least the tiniest bit wistful? *Make up your mind! Do you want to be matrimonial prey or…?*

No *or*. There was no other option.

'So, this afternoon proved surprising, huh?'

She could say that again.

'I didn't expect your father to be so generous. When I saw the chopper, I thought he might be after blood—mainly mine.'

He rested his head back. 'I'm starting to wonder if I ever knew my father at all. This morning I found out I've been mistaken about him since I was fourteen.'

'Mistaken how?'

He turned his head to meet her gaze. 'At the age of fourteen I overheard something and I completely misinterpreted it.' He related the conversation he and Fraser had had earlier. She listened in silence, her eyes going wide. 'Fact is, Charlie, the man I knew before then was always hard and demanding, but he could be generous too. He was never demonstrative, didn't make a big song and dance about things, liked to keep things low-key, but he was never cruel or vengeful. This afternoon *shouldn't* have surprised me.'

She leaned towards him. 'For all of these years you didn't think he *wanted* you at Kings Reach?'

Trust her to latch on to the most significant part of what he'd just said.

He shrugged and her face softened. 'Oh, Tom. Why didn't you talk to anyone about it?'

It had cut too deep, that was why. And… 'Communication has never been Fraser's strong point.' He rolled his shoulders. 'His sons are carrying on the tradition, I guess.'

'So that's been the main source of tension between the two of you over the years?'

One-sided tension, he now saw. To know he'd been so mistaken shifted things, changed his perspective. 'Will died two months after that. And I blamed him for Will's death—we all did.'

But he'd started to see that some of the viciousness of his blame had also originated from how betrayed and let-down he'd felt by Fraser in the lead-up to that time. And why he felt so strongly about Fraser's desire to break the irrevocable trust now.

Charlie set her glass down, a frown in her eyes.

'I thought Will's death was an accident. Why would you blame Fraser for it?'

His heart pounded in sick thuds. 'It was, but it was a preventable one. If Fraser hadn't lost his temper, Will would still be alive today.'

CHAPTER TWELVE

Charlie went hot, and then cold all over. She wanted to cry at the expression on Tom's face. She moved to sit beside him, slipped her hand inside his. 'Oh, Tom, what a weight to bear. For all of you.' She didn't know if she should ask or not, but he'd just admitted communication wasn't his strength. And just like his mistaken belief that Fraser hadn't wanted him at the station, had Tom not spoken to anyone about *this* either?

'What happened?' If he didn't want to talk about it he could shut her down, and she'd respect that. But some sixth sense told her he *needed* to talk about it. Saying the words out loud might help lance them of their poison.

His head dropped back and he stared at the ceiling as if unutterably weary. 'It was the end of the dry season—and it was *really* dry that year. The wet was late, the heat was relentless and emotions were running high.'

Few things were worse out here than the big wet arriving late. The grasses dried up and crumbled to dust, the creeks disappeared and the rivers became trickles; stock started to die from lack of water, lack of food. Throw in the lightning strikes from storm clouds that promised so much but retreated north back out to sea, leaving nothing but wildfires in their wake…and things became tense, dire.

Out here, that worry became an obsession—all-consuming. Tempers frayed, fear took hold, and stations went under. But what did any of that have to do with Will's accident?

'The five of us boys were out with Dad in one of the big work utes. We all knew he was worried, but we were just kids, so we were fooling around as usual.' He swallowed. 'We came across three steers in a bad way. They were too far gone to save. Dad had to put them down.'

She nodded. 'It's a horrible thing to have to do.'

'We were quiet for a bit afterwards—respecting that—but… I remember feeling suffocated, as if the tension and suspense of waiting for the dry to break had lasted forever. When I was a kid, Charlie, I liked to make people laugh, liked to lighten the moment.'

Couldn't he see he still did that?

'So much of that day is burned on my memory. But for the life of me I can't remember what joke or flip comment it was that I made. I know it got a laugh from the other boys. Not belly laughs, just snorts and sniggers, but it rubbed Fraser up the wrong way and he snapped at me. *"Show some respect and act your age!"'*

'You were fourteen, right?' She rolled her eyes. 'That *was* you acting your age.'

He huffed out a laugh. 'Exactly. So far everything was progressing along predictable lines—we'd all danced this dance before. But then Will, who was always kind of quiet and dreamy, piped up with, "C'mon, Dad, pull your head in. You have to admit that was pretty funny." It was *so* unexpected the rest of us boys just exploded—completely lost it. Belly laughed, the whole kit and caboodle.'

He grinned as if remembering that moment and it stole her breath.

'No doubt a part of our reaction was the break in tension that had gripped us for weeks.' He rubbed a hand over his jaw. 'I wish to God Dad had been able to see the funny side.'

Except Fraser had just put down three animals—a station worker's most hated job. He'd probably been consumed with worry about the welfare of the rest of his stock.

'Dad exploded too, but with anger. He ordered Will into the tray of the ute for a time-out. It wasn't that unusual for any of us to travel in the tray of the ute—we liked it. The wind in our hair and all that. But it was a blisteringly hot day…'

He paused and she squeezed his hand.

'Jack told Dad he was being an idiot, overreacting, and joined Will in the tray. Which put Dad in an even worse temper.'

She winced.

Tom didn't say anything for a long moment, his expression growing grimmer. She had to fight the urge to brush the hair out of his eyes. A gesture like that would be far too intimate, and they were *just friends*.

He wouldn't mind if you seduced him, though.

She slammed a lid on that thought.

'Fraser never drove fast when any of us were in the tray. I don't think he would've that day either, but in his temper he did initially accelerate faster than he normally would've done.' The remaining colour leached from his face. 'One wheel hit a pothole, another wheel shot over a rock and…' He shook his head. 'Will was so little and he went sailing out of the tray…'

Her heart pounded.

'He should've ended up with a few bruises, nothing more. At worse a broken arm. Instead he landed funny and broke his neck.'

She pressed a hand to her mouth, her eyes burning.

'I remember Jack cradling Will in his arms yelling, "What have you done? What have you done?" over and over at Fraser.' His voice cracked. 'We all knew—one look at the angle of Will's neck and… So wrong.' Grief pulled at his face. 'I didn't know what to do. I wrapped an arm around Fitz. He'd gone as still as Will—had completely shut down. Logan came up on Fitz's other side, and we just stood there with our arms around each other.'

He shook himself, as if freeing his head from a bad dream. 'I don't remember much after that—just flashes. Shock, I suppose. What I do know is that nothing was the same afterwards. Jack left. Fitz retreated into himself. Mum went into mourning, and Fraser threw himself into work. I don't know how to explain it,' a shudder rippled through him, 'but I feel as if we lost something even more precious that day than just Will.'

She couldn't stem the tears streaming down her cheeks. Kneeling beside him, she wrapped her arms around his shoulders and held him tight. 'Oh, Tom, your poor family.'

Strong arms curved around her waist and he dragged her into his lap and buried his face in her hair. They remained like that for a long time. Had anyone held him like this at the time? Knowing Tom, with Jack gone he'd have thrown himself into the practicalities of looking after his mother and little brothers.

He eased away and she reluctantly loosened her grip. 'Your family make it look so easy, Charlie.'

'What?'

'Being a family. We were like that once—not a carbon copy, but strong in our own way. I want that for Bea.' He touched a finger to her cheek. 'Your Pop lied to you and yet you forgave him just—' he clicked his fingers '—like magic! And things were made right.'

She shook her head. 'Not magic.'

Tom wanted a family like she had—a supportive family who stuck with each other through thick and thin. And he didn't want it just for Bea but himself too, even if he couldn't see that. He just didn't think it was achievable.

'There's nothing magical about it, Tom. We talk, even when it's hard. We accept the fact that we'll all make mistakes. We apologise when we're wrong, and we forgive each other—even when we don't want to. Maybe especially when we don't want to.'

'You think I should forgive Fraser?'

She turned the question over in her mind. She had definite opinions on the matter, but she was equally certain she shouldn't voice them. 'What do you think?'

He stared at a point in the distance. 'I know he didn't mean for the accident to happen. I know if he could, he'd go back and change it.' His lips twisted. 'Since having Bea, I know firsthand how one's patience can be stretched so thin it becomes almost non-existent.'

'There were days I'd have cheerfully fed the Dudleys to the dingoes.'

He laughed, but sobered a moment later. 'I can't begin to imagine the hell Fraser has been through. I know he felt responsible, and in hindsight I can see he must've felt as if we were all ranged against him.'

Maybe they had been, and that was understandable, but… '*Can* you forgive him?'

'I…' He shook his head, frowning. 'I already

have. I don't even know when that happened.' He grimaced. 'And now I suppose I have to find a way to *communicate* that to him.'

Her insides turned to mush. She pressed a hand to his cheek. 'You're a good man, Tom.' And then she reached up and kissed him.

Tom kissed her back—*thoroughly*. Easing away, she sucked her bottom lip into her mouth. She ought to force herself off his lap and put some distance between them, but she couldn't move.

Hunger flared in his eyes. Cradling the back of her head in his large hand, he pulled her in for another kiss—hot and intense—and with a groan she threw her arms around his neck and kissed him back with all of herself. Nothing had ever felt more right than kissing Tom.

The heat and need simmering between them for the last few weeks flared now. Straddling his lap, she pressed herself against the bulge in his jeans, breaking off with a gasp when he pushed her shirt up and sucked one turgid nipple into his mouth through the flimsy material of her bra until she was writhing with need and want. Strong hands clamped to her hips to hold her still. 'If you want me to stop, Charlie—'

'Shut up,' she growled, 'and don't stop.'

'I love a woman who knows what she wants.'

Love? Her heart leapt.

Don't be stupid. That's just hormones talking.

'Hold on.'

He rose and she wrapped her legs around his hips. 'Why didn't I wear a dress?' she groaned.

Firm fingers dug into her buttocks, making her want to whimper and beg. 'Wear one for me tomorrow?'

'Deal.' She'd promise him anything in this moment. 'If you get me out of these clothes as fast as you can.'

In the bedroom, he did exactly that. They spent no time admiring each other's nakedness, though. Falling to the bed, their bodies came together in a thunderclap. She hooked her heels behind his back and with his hands beneath her buttocks he pulled her so close she felt as if she were a part of him. When she came, stars burst behind her eyelids.

Charlie blinked herself awake the next morning to find Tom staring at her, a frown in his eyes—a frown that spread across his entire face. She immediately frowned back. 'Why are you frowning at me?'

'Why are you frowning at me?' he countered, moving higher up in the bed. She did too, bringing the sheet with her to cover her nakedness.

'You were frowning at me first.' She folded her arms over the sheet, wondering why everything felt so suddenly awkward after the perfection of their lovemaking last night. 'Besides you're the one who needs to practise their communication skills.' She wanted to leap out of bed and run away. 'So…go on.'

'It's just…' His frown deepened. 'We said we weren't going to do this again.'

Did he regret it? Scrubbing both hands over her face, she nodded. 'That is what we agreed.' A cold fist tightened about her heart. She liked Tom. She liked him a lot. But he wasn't sticking around. He'd be heading back to Sydney soon and he had no intention of asking her to join him there. He'd made *that* very clear.

You don't want to join him.

Her mouth went dry. She didn't *want* to want that. She didn't want her heart shattered into a million little fragments. She didn't want to lie awake at night aching for him and wondering where he was, what he was doing, and who he was doing it with. She didn't want to throb and ache and yearn until everything hurt. She didn't want to feel so empty she could no longer see the beauty around her.

Panic propelled her out of bed, nakedness and all. She threw on the first thing she found—his shirt. Fumbling with the buttons, she swung back to face him. 'Fine, we made a mistake.'

His head rocked back.

'Last night got heavy and intense pretty fast. You're so beautiful, Tom, and making love with you is glorious.'

He started to laugh and something in his eyes gentled. 'Slow down, Charlie.'

She couldn't afford to slow down! If she slowed down he might break her heart. 'We *can't* let it happen again. You're a city boy. You'll be going back to Sydney soon and you said you had no room in your life—' she planted her hands on her hips and pulled out the big guns '—or *Bea's* life, for someone like me.'

He didn't rocket out of bed in a panic as she'd done, but at Bea's name everything about him went on high alert. 'Someone like you?'

'A lover. A potential romantic interest.'

He didn't deny it and things inside of her started to droop, which made no sense. Because she hadn't fallen in love with him. *She hadn't.* 'Don't worry, Tom, I haven't read anything into last night. Despite my family's attempts at matchmaking, a match hasn't been made. You can rest easy.'

He still didn't say anything and she threw her hands in the air. 'And now I have to find a dress to wear!'

Epiphanies kept coming at Tom, thick and fast. Epiphany Number One: He'd fallen in love with Charlie. How the hell had that happened?

Act natural. Don't swear.

'Keep your shirt on, Charlie.' He said it because he had to say something—and because he didn't want to sit quietly with this new knowledge while she stared at him like that. '*My* shirt,' he added with a grin, when grinning was the last thing he felt like doing. Her eyes narrowed as if she didn't trust his levity. 'Ditch the dress. Wear your usual jeans. We wouldn't want you to act out of character and give your family any false hopes, now, would we?'

Had that sounded bitter? Probably. Because of Epiphany Number Two: Charlie didn't love him back.

At the exact moment he'd realised *he'd fallen in love with her*, Charlie had opened her eyes and frowned at him and he'd realised she *didn't love him back*. He now had two options. He could either make a fool of himself and tell her he loved her—which wouldn't change the fact that she didn't love him—or he could work at getting things back to normal as if nothing had changed.

He chose option two. He didn't think he'd be able to cope with her sympathy and pity, or her apologies. Maybe she'd lash out at him instead— remind him they'd promised to keep things light. That thought didn't fill him with enthusiasm either. He shoved down the roaring ache that fought to scrabble free. He couldn't give way to it now.

'Why don't you take the first shower?'

She left without another word. After she'd finished in the bathroom, he went in himself. He stood beneath hot needles of water, hands clenching and unclenching, eyes and throat burning. He'd promised to never fall in love again. What the hell had he been thinking, messing with Charlie like that? Had he really thought…?

Pull yourself together.

He turned the hot tap off and gritted his teeth against the sudden blast of cold. He had responsibilities. He had to look after Bea, the irrevocable trust—his brothers were depending on him. He could feel sorry for himself later.

Striding into the kitchen, he found Charlie slumped over a mug of coffee. Reaching for the pot, she poured him one and pushed it across the table. Couldn't she even manage a smile?

He didn't sit. Seizing his mug, he took a sip and then gestured towards the front door. 'Ready?' They'd promised to breakfast with the rest of the family.

'I don't think so.' Her eyes travelled over him, her gaze narrowing. 'Not when you look like that.'

'Like what?'

She slammed her mug to the table. 'What are you so grumpy about? What did I say that's annoyed you so much?'

'You really want to know?'

'Absolutely!'

Did his eyes flash as fiercely as hers? 'The way you said I'm a *city boy*. You said it as if it was the most pathetic, ugliest, most detestable thing on earth.'

Her jaw dropped. 'I did not!'

'*Yes*, you did. But I'm not your father, Charlie, and I'm not your rotter of an ex-boyfriend.' What had stung the most this morning wasn't anything she'd said, but her panic. Not that he had any intention of revealing that. Was she really *that* afraid of getting involved with him? 'I don't cheat or lie or break my promises. I'm not cruel to animals or people.' What else had been on her list of things that had made her angry?

She grimaced. 'And you're not mean. I'm sorry. I didn't want to make you feel pathetic or ugly or detestable. You're none of those things.'

Her apology had his outrage evaporating. 'I know you didn't. I…' He rubbed a hand over his face. 'Fact is, being back in the Kimberley has been great.' And in large part he had her to thank for that. She'd reminded him of all the reasons he loved the place.

'What's wrong with that?'

'I feel as if I've found a missing piece of myself.'

She leaned across the table towards him. A pulse at the base of her throat pounded. 'You're thinking of coming back?'

'Working remotely these last few weeks has made me see how I could make it work. Given that we've slept together *twice*—' she flinched and he bit back a curse '—I need to know if you'd find it awkward living next door to me?'

Her mouth opened and closed but not a single word emerged.

Recalling her panic as she'd bolted out of bed this morning, he went cold all over. 'Nothing else has changed,' he ground out—just so she knew—

because nothing else *had* changed. She didn't love him. And he had no intention of embarking on a relationship with a woman who'd made it insultingly clear that sleeping with him had been a mistake!

'So we'd just be neighbours?'

He didn't understand the edge to her voice. 'Just neighbours. Who live five hours away from each other.' He didn't know why he added that last bit. Other than the fact that reminding her of the distance might allay her *panic*.

She folded her arms with infuriating calm, but her eyes blazed. 'And how long do you expect me to continue being Bea's nanny?'

He pretended to mull that over, but inside him things went hard. 'From memory you weren't interested in spending much time in the city and there'll be a transition period over the next few months, so...' He crossed one ankle over the other as if he didn't have a care in the world. He didn't understand why it was so important he look relaxed and easy—pride perhaps, and wanting to save face—but he had no intention of giving her the satisfaction of losing his cool.

Can you hear yourself?

Shut up!

'With Dad finally leasing you the land, you'll be needed here. So why don't we bring an end to that contract right now? Bea and I will leave and you can stay here.'

She pushed away from the table. 'Don't tell me

what to do or where I'm *needed*. You've no idea what our situation is here.'

Nor would he get a chance to. A void opened up inside him.

'The wage I'm pulling this season will be of more use to my family than having me here to help out. And that's besides the fact that my horses, dogs and truck are all still at Kings Reach.'

His face twisted. 'And that's what really matters to you, Charlie, isn't it? Your safe little world with your horses and dogs and trucks. They mean more to you than people.'

She stared at him as if he made no sense.

'Well, here's something else for you to chew over. If you love someone, then surely *they* should matter more to you than where you damn well live!'

Her head snapped back.

'Bea and I will be returning to Kings Reach after breakfast. I'll send the chopper for you tomorrow. Enjoy some extra time with your family. On me. Now I'm starved.' He slammed his hat to his head. 'I'm going to breakfast.'

He stomped across to the main house, his heart slumping to his feet. What the hell had he just done?

And yet in his mind's eye all he could see was the panic racing across Charlie's face in bed this morning. The sooner he ended their arrangement, the better.

CHAPTER THIRTEEN

'*No!*' Bea shouted when Tom told her they'd be returning to Kings Reach after breakfast. 'Charlie promised to show me the waterhole and Nanna said she'd teach me how to make meringues, and I want to meet Bubbles and Colette and Godfrey.'

Who?

'Charlie's old pony, our goat and the oak tree,' Sid told him.

'You have an oak?'

Don't get distracted.

Tom pinched the bridge of his nose and counted to three. 'We can come back another day.'

'I want to stay *now*!'

Did kids instinctively know when a parent's patience was at its thinnest? Was it a superpower or something? 'Sorry, Bea, but I have things I need to do.'

Bea stuck her bottom lip out and glared. 'I'm not—'

'You are,' he shot back with a growl. Bea's eyes widened before filling with tears. He instantly felt like a heel.

'Or,' Vicky said, 'Bea can stay here for another night and go home with Charlie in the morning. We'd love to have her, Tom.'

He glanced at Vicky, who silently mouthed *Go on* with an encouraging nod. He pushed his chair back and patted his knee. Bea was up on it in an instant. He thumbed away a tear from her cheek. 'How do you feel about that plan, Buzzy Bea?'

She nodded.

'I'm sorry I snapped. I'm disappointed I can't stay and meet Bubbles and Godfrey and Colette too.'

Gutted, actually. He'd give anything for Charlie to welcome him here—for her to beg him to stay.

Bea flung her arms around his neck and he hugged her tight. Charlie chose that moment to enter the kitchen. 'Okay, Bea.' He eased away, dragging his gaze from Charlie, who looked predictably delectable in worn denim jeans, her every curve displayed to glorious perfection. It felt like a taunt, though he knew she didn't mean it that way. 'You'll stay here and have all the fun with Charlie and can tell me all about it when you get back to Kings Reach tomorrow. Promise to do everything Charlie, Auntie Vicky and Nanna tell you to do.'

The *Auntie* and *Nanna* rolled off his tongue far too easily—as if it was only natural for Bea and him to be welcomed so easily into Charlie's family and find a place there.

Wishful thinking.

'Will you be scared to go in the helicopter tomorrow?'

Bea shook her head. 'Charlie will be with me.'

Whatever else, he knew his little girl would be safe with Charlie. What an idiot he'd been to think a third person would ruin his and Bea's cosy little circle. Not Charlie. She'd somehow made it complete.

The family gathered to wave him off. As he drove away, though, it wasn't the family tableau but the panic that had flashed in Charlie's eyes this morning that played over and over in his mind.

Charlie stared after the car. Tom even had the audacity to stick a hand out of the window and give a jaunty wave. It was all she could do to keep the scowl from her face. What the hell was his problem?

Nanna took Bea back inside. Mum moved up behind Charlie. 'Everything okay?'

'Apparently not.' She lifted her hands, let them drop. 'I've no idea what his problem is.'

A shrewd eyebrow lifted. 'You sure about that?'

'I...'

What had she said or done this morning that had set him off, that had changed everything? Her throat ached. Her chest ached. Had he really just fired her? Was her adventure with him and Bea at an end?

She didn't want it to be at an end. Even given her righteous anger against Fraser and her worry for Pop and Melaleuca Downs, these last few weeks had been… She swallowed. They'd been the best fun of her life. Watching Tom drive away had felt like losing her best friend.

'Charlie?'

She shook herself. 'He said something to me and…' *If you loved someone, shouldn't they matter more than where you lived?* The words had become burrs beneath her skin that she couldn't shift. 'He didn't make *any* sense.'

'Will you do me a favour, Charlie?'

She turned. 'Of course.'

'Starlight's action seems a bit off to me. Would you take her out and let me know what you think?'

Charlie was an excellent horsewoman, but her mother was a better one.

'Just fifteen minutes out to the fairy grove and back. It shouldn't take longer than half an hour tops.'

The fairy grove was a pretty spot along the river, ringed with weeping willows. They'd called it that ever since Charlie was a little girl and said it reminded her of a picture in her book of fairy tales.

'I find a good canter allways clears my head.' Vicky patted her arm and returned to the house. Charlie headed for the stables.

She cantered, but no matter what she did, she couldn't lose herself in it the way she normally did. For no reason at all tears burned her eyes, but the wind dried them before they could fall. And if tears didn't fall they weren't tears at all, right?

She went over the morning's events and tried to work out what had happened, where it had all gone so wrong. She'd woken to find Tom frowning at her. *Frowning*. Not the best start to the day!

When she'd reminded him that she hadn't forgotten that he *didn't* want a romantic entanglement—in an attempt to dislodge his frown—he hadn't contradicted her. He *had* looked disgruntled, though. Which was the bit that didn't make sense. She'd done her absolute best to assuage any fears he might've harboured, and instead of being grateful he'd become offended about the city-boy thing.

She and Starlight reached the fairy grove and even its beauty couldn't soothe the burn in her soul. Turning Starlight's head for home, she cantered back, her mind no clearer than before, but her agitation quieter for the exercise and fresh air.

The waterhole was a ten-minute drive from the house and she and Bea headed there once she returned from her ride. Bea stared at the wide sandy beach, clear shallows, and rock pools with the wide-eyed awe of a five-year-old and declared it, 'The best place in the whole world.'

Bea explored and kept up a constant flow of chatter. Charlie managed to keep up, though half of her mind remained on Tom and his baffling behaviour. It was while they were coming up with reasons why ladybird had spots on their wings that the real reason she'd leaped out of bed this morning hit her.

It hadn't been Tom's fears she'd been trying to allay, but her own!

She thumped down to a rock, breathing hard. She'd fallen in love with Tom. She glanced across to where Bea crouched down, poking the water with a stick. And his daughter.

Despite her best intentions, she'd fallen in love with a man who had no intention of sticking around. Correction, he might stick around, but he had no intention of sticking with *her*. He'd told her *that* more than once. What was she, a masochist?

But Tom had filled her life with laughter and fun and understanding. He'd fought on her side against his father, even though she'd been wrong. He'd offered her support and comfort and he hadn't blamed her for her mistakes. *And* he made love like an angel. She *loved* him.

Her head dropped to her knees. But he didn't love her back. And there was nothing she could do about it.

She frowned and lifted her head, their conversation this morning playing through her mind. Then why had he taken offence at the 'city boy' comment? Why had he thrown that 'if you love someone they should matter more than where you live' at her? It had come out of *nowhere*.

Her frown deepened. And why on earth had he fired her?

Unless…

Her heart gave a giant kick. Did he have feelings for her too? If she could change her mind, then so could he.

'I'm a woman of action, not a cowpat,' she murmured, shooting to her feet. 'Hey, Bea, did I tell you that, if you ask nicely, Auntie Vicky would probably teach you some fancy hopscotch moves?'

Bea was at her side in seconds. 'And then I might beat you.'

'Well, you could give it a red-hot go.'

Bea started jumping up and down. 'Can we go ask her?'

An hour and a half into the drive, Tom slammed the car to a halt, a single thought crystallising in his mind. *He'd* frowned at *her*. When Charlie had woken this morning, he'd been frowning at her.

He'd been convinced that she'd recognised his feelings—that they must be plastered all over his face—and that was why she'd panicked, but… She'd been half-asleep. What if his frown had made her think he'd regretted the night they'd spent together? What if his frown had caused her to panic?

His mouth went dry. What if he'd completely misinterpreted the events of this morning, the way he had so many years ago with his father?

He thumped the steering wheel and called himself every rude name he could think of.

He wasn't making the same mistake again!

Gritting his teeth, he turned the car around and headed back to Melaleuca. 'What are you—a cowpat?' he spat. Had he really turned tail and run because he'd been too afraid to tell a girl he loved her? Because maybe she didn't love him back? His brothers would laugh their heads off if they ever found out. He'd never live it down. He wouldn't *deserve* to live it down.

Charlie might not love him, but he'd damn well give her a chance to tell him that herself. At least then he'd know. And that had to be better than *this*.

Forty minutes into his drive back to Melaleuca, dust rose up ahead of him from a car travelling towards him in the opposite direction. It took the two cars three minutes to reach one another, and for every single one of those minutes, the ball of tension beneath his breastbone grew, though he didn't know why. The two cars would pass and continue on their way.

The car screeched to a halt before it reached him, though, and the driver shot out like a rocket to stand in the middle of the road, hands on hips.

His jaw dropped. *Charlie?*

Bea? Had something happened? He slammed on the brakes, the car skidding to a halt. He shot out of it and made a beeline for Charlie. 'Is everything—?'

'You can just shut up and listen to me for a moment, Thomas Benedick King!'

Electricity bristled and crackled from her as if embedded in her skin, and the expression in her eyes could blister paint from walls. He held up his hands and wisely kept his mouth shut. If anything had happened to Bea she'd be devastated, not angry. She wasn't here to give him bad news. At least, not *that* kind of bad news.

'You do *not* get to tell me what to do or where I belong or…or what to do!'

He kept an eye on the finger she jabbed at him. Talk about formidable. Talk about magnificent!

'You don't get to throw a hissy fit and then walk away without giving me the right of reply.'

'Not fair,' he agreed, because it appeared she finally expected him to say something.

'Damn right,' she muttered.

'Charlie—'

'No!' She pointed that finger at him again and he promptly closed his mouth. 'I woke up this morning to find you looking like the world had come to an end.'

'It wasn't that bad.' He rolled his shoulders. 'I—'

Her face darkened and she advanced on him.

'Like the end of the world,' he agreed in a rush, fascinated to see this new side of her.

'So I,' she clapped a hand to her chest, 'like some stupid little Bambi, did my best to ease your concerns as soon as I could, to let you know

I hadn't read more into our encounter than you were comfortable with, in an attempt to get things back to normal.'

He snorted. Nothing about this morning had been normal.

'But instead of being relieved or having the grace to show some gratitude and appreciation…' She whirled away, throwing her arms up.

Did she seriously think he didn't appreciate her?

She spun back. '*Noooo*, instead you took offence. And fired me!'

A huge mistake. 'Charlie…'

That finger jabbed in his general direction again. 'But that's not happening, you hear me? You're not firing me just like that.'

He was glad to hear it, but—

'Your little girl really likes me and she'll need a transition period.' She squared her chin. 'And I really like her, so…so do I.'

How would she feel about a transition period of forever?

She shook out her arms and legs as if trying to shake off her fury. He clenched his hands to stop from reaching for her. 'Is it okay if I say something now?'

She nodded and shrugged as if she didn't care what he did or said, but he was a father of a five-year-old, and, while Charlie might be far more complicated than a five-year-old, he saw through her bluster—saw through to the vulnerable heart of her. What he said and did now mattered to them both. It might not mean love and forever, but Charlie wasn't indifferent to him. That was something he could work with, build on.

First, though, he had to undo the hurt he'd caused her today. 'I want to apologise for how I behaved this morning. It was stupid and irrational and unfair.' He backed up to lean against the bonnet of his car. She followed, keeping the same amount of distance between them, standing with her legs planted firmly and her arms crossed. His heart thrashed around in his ribcage. 'I'm sorry.'

'Tom—'

'No.' He thumped a hand to his chest. 'My turn.'

She swallowed. 'Okay.'

All of the morning's pain poured through him again and he couldn't keep it locked behind the walls of his heart. His heart no longer had walls. 'The thing is, you did *too* good a job at easing my so-called concerns.'

She moistened her lips. 'So-called?'

'Charlie, you were easing the wrong concerns.'

She bit her thumb. 'Wrong how?' Pulling it from her mouth, she glared at him. 'What *were* your concerns?'

His hands went clammy and a lump the size of a tractor lodged in his throat.

'Tom?'

'My concerns,' he grated out, 'were the…*exact* opposite.'

He watched her take that in, mull it over and finally nod. He supposed he ought to be grateful that she didn't flinch or turn away…that sympathy didn't flood her eyes. Caught on the edge of a precipice, he held his breath and prayed the roll of the dice would fall his way.

'So you *do* have feelings,' she said cautiously.

He stared at her and the world went dark and the damn dice rolled into a black chasm of nothingness. He sagged against the car. 'You did know, then?' His first instincts had been correct. 'When you woke this morning. You realised and—'

'What? *No.* I didn't work it out until I was down at the waterhole with Bea.'

A chink of light appeared in the darkness. 'But you panicked—this morning. You leapt out of bed and totally freaked out, and I thought it was because you could see in my face that I'd developed feelings for you.'

'I panicked because you were frowning at me and I realised I'd caught feelings for you.'

Her words punched the breath from his body. He couldn't do or say anything.

'And you were frowning as if last night had been the biggest mistake of your life!'

'I was frowning because that was the exact moment I realised I'd—' how had she phrased it? '—caught feelings for you.'

She'd started pacing, but halted now. Very slowly she turned.

He shrugged. 'I was gobsmacked. It took me completely by surprise. I was trying to sort out what it meant. *That's* when you opened your eyes.'

The beginnings of a smile played across her lips. 'Caught feelings, huh?'

'Big time,' he assured her.

She moved towards him, a slow, sexy saunter that had his skin stretching tight. She gave his shoulder a playful push. 'So you like me, huh?'

He reached for her hand and reeled her in until he had her captured in the circle of his arms. 'My feelings for you are bigger than dinosaurs and the Sydney Harbour Bridge and blue whales *combined.*'

'That big?' She feigned being impressed.

Resting his forehead against hers, he felt as if he'd finally arrived home. 'I love you to the moon and back, Charlie.'

Her eyes turned soft and dewy. 'That far, huh?'

'That far.' With Charlie he'd found something that fulfilled all of his old idealistic dreams about love and romance. When he'd least expected to. But he meant to cherish it. He meant to cherish *her.*

She sobered. 'I love you more than the Kimberley, Tom. I love you more than Melaleuca Downs. You're right—the *who* matters far more than the *where.* I'll follow you to the end of the world if I have to.'

She meant it. He didn't doubt that for a moment. But she had a lot of other people out here that she loved too. And so did he.

She wrinkled her nose. 'But please don't make me follow you to Antarctica. I hate the cold.'

He gave a bark of laughter and then they were both grinning madly at each other. 'We *are* home, Charlie. I want to make a home here with you in the Kimberley.'

'You don't have to.'

'I want to. Besides, Bea informed me the other day that we were moving here because she refused to be parted from Rambo or Uncle Fitz, and also informed me that you'd help her pack up all her things in Sydney.'

'She's got it all sorted, then?'

He nodded. 'And speaking of Bea...'

'Back at Melaleuca, either getting hopscotch lessons from Mum or making meringues with Nan. I'm not expected back until late and I checked with Bea that she was okay with that.' Catching her bottom lip between her teeth, she glanced up at him from beneath her eyelashes and moved suggestively against him. Air hissed out of his lungs. 'I have a picnic rug in the car and Nan sent me off with a lot of provisions. We could have a picnic—' she waggled her eyebrows suggestively '—before we head back.'

He glanced at her car and then back at her. 'You came after me to tell me you loved me?'

'When it hit me that you might've caught feelings too, well... I'm a woman of action—'

'Not a cowpat,' they finished in unison.

She glanced at his car and frowned. 'Why were you heading back to the Downs? What did you forget?'

'You, Charlie. I forgot you.'

She visibly melted. 'Well, now that you have me, Tom, what do you mean to do with me?'

'Now, *that*, Charlie—' his head lowered to hers '—is something I can't wait to show you.'

They kissed and it held all the heat and passion that he hungered for, but also something deeper—a love that filled his heart so full he thought he might burst. Lifting his head long moments later, he met her gaze. 'I'm never letting you go, Charlie.'

'I'm never letting you go times ten,' she whispered back.

Their lips met again, fiercer, more joyful and exuberant. It was a long time before they had their picnic.

* * * * *

Get up to 4 Free Books!

We'll send you 2 free books from each series you try
PLUS a free Mystery Gift.

Both the **Harlequin® Historical** and **Harlequin® Romance** series feature compelling novels filled with emotion and simmering romance.

YES! Please send me 2 FREE novels from the Harlequin Historical or Harlequin Romance series and my FREE Mystery Gift (gift is worth about $10 retail). I may cancel anytime by emailing ReaderServiceInfo@Harlequin.com or by calling 1-800-873-8635. If I don't cancel, I will receive 5 new Harlequin Historical books every month and be billed just $6.39 each in the U.S. or $7.19 each in Canada, or 4 new Harlequin Romance Larger-Print books every month and be billed just $7.19 each in the U.S. or $7.99 each in Canada, a savings of 20% off the cover price. It's quite a bargain! Shipping and handling is just 75¢ per book in the U.S. and $1.75 per book in Canada.* I understand that accepting the free books and gift places me under no obligation to buy anything—they are mine to keep for free no matter what I decide.

Choose one:
- ☐ Harlequin Historical (246/349 BPA G3CD)
- ☐ Harlequin Romance Larger-Print (119/319 BPA G3CD)
- ☐ Or Try Both! (246/349 & 119/319 BPA G3CE)

Name (please print)

Address   Apt. #

City   State/Province   Zip/Postal Code

Email: Please check this box ☐ if you would like to receive newsletters and promotional emails from Harlequin Enterprises ULC and its affiliates. You can unsubscribe anytime.

Mail to the Harlequin Reader Service:
IN U.S.A.: P.O. Box 1341, Buffalo, NY 14240-8531
IN CANADA: P.O. Box 603, Fort Erie, Ontario L2A 5X3

Want to explore our other series or interested in ebooks? Visit www.ReaderService.com or call 1-800-873-8635.

*Terms and prices subject to change without notice. Prices do not include sales taxes, which will be charged (if applicable) based on your state or country of residence. Canadian residents will be charged applicable taxes. Offer not valid in Quebec. This offer is limited to one order per household. Books received may not be as shown. Not valid for current subscribers to the Harlequin Historical or Harlequin Romance series. All orders subject to approval. Credit or debit balances in a customer's account(s) may be offset by any other outstanding balance owed by or to the customer. Please allow 4 to 6 weeks for delivery. Offer available while quantities last.

Your Privacy — Your information is being collected by Harlequin Enterprises ULC, operating as Harlequin Reader Service. For a complete summary of the information we collect, how we use this information and to whom it is disclosed, please visit our privacy notice located at https://corporate.harlequin.com/privacy-notice. Notice to California Residents—Under California law, you have specific rights to control and access your data. For more information on these rights and how to exercise them, visit https://corporate.harlequin.com/california-privacy. For additional information for residents of other U.S. states that provide their residents with certain rights with respect to personal data, visit https://corporate.harlequin.com/other-state-residents-privacy-rights.

HHHRLP2603

"What are you talking about?"

Olivia gestured vaguely, her hand flapping uselessly toward all the bare skin. "*This.* You. Taking off your clothes."

Nyla blinked, then finally laughed, low and throaty. "Oh my God, Olivia. I'm not stripping down for a skinny-dip. I'm preparing to swim the last few yards out to the enclosure. I'm not about to drag my jeans through salt water."

Olivia's mouth opened. Closed. Opened again. "Right. Of course. Obviously."

Her voice had gone higher than a prepubescent boy's, and she could *feel* the heat rising in her face, but there was no stopping it now. Nyla was still smiling, all sharp-eyed and *smug*.

She flipped the goggles down over her head and slung a backpack on. "You coming," Nyla asked, smirking, "or are you just going to sit there and stare at me all morning?"

"Staring's...a real option right about now," Olivia blurted out.

And when Nyla dove cleanly beneath the surface, Olivia sat there gripping the straps of her jumper, her heart hammering out a staccato rhythm, as she muttered under her breath, "Yikes. I'm in trouble."

Dear Reader,

When a ransomware attack strikes the Sea Turtle Research and Education Center, Dr. Nyla Dávila's life's work hangs in the balance. But when the university brings in outside help, she finds herself working alongside Olivia Navarro, a brilliant but irreverent cybersecurity expert, whose arrival feels like both an intrusion and an unexpected spark.

Readers of my first book series, The Navarros, may remember Olivia. She's cousin to Val, Rafi and Nati Navarro, appearing alongside Val in the very first pages of *A Delicious Dilemma*. I've long wanted to tell her story, and I'm delighted to bring her to the forefront here.

Olivia has built her career proving herself in a world that doesn't easily trust outsiders or queer women who break the rules to get results. But nothing could have prepared her for Nyla, whose fierce dedication to her research is matched only by the vulnerability she keeps carefully guarded. Amid the backdrop of sea turtle rescues and starlit beaches, two women must decide if they're willing to risk their hearts for something far more uncertain than science or programming code: love.

Best,

Sera